PUBLIC OFFERINGS

Book Two

The Price of a Life

A novel by

Bob LiVolsi

NOTICE

This is a work of fiction. Names, characters, places, events, and
incidents are either products of the author's imagination or used
fictitiously. Any resemblance to actual persons, living or dead, is purely
coincidental.

DEDICATION

To Susan who has patiently believed in me and encouraged me for far too long for her own good. Thank you, my darling wife, for being there always and for loving me. I love you always.

To all the people in generous communities of caring around the world who continue to sacrifice their comfort and often risk their lives to bring hope to our peers in less fortunate corners of the world. And to the people of Sierra Leone whose misery at the hands of warlords and power brokers informed the very first draft of this book all those years ago in 1995. Even at this writing, the struggles of the Leoneans and other West Africans continue as they deal with the largest Ebola outbreak yet recorded.

To all those who cling to and proclaim a faith of compassion for our human beings, built on service not conquest, built on hope not rules, and encompassed by love – at all times recognizing a much greater force that transcends our personal demands and yet embraces our free will and individuality.

TABLE OF CONTENTS

SUMMARY OF BIRTHRIGHT: BOOK ONE   vii

BOOK TWO – Price of a Life

October 22

    CHAPTER 1 – Southeastern Sierra Leone   3

    CHAPTER 2 – Chicago: O'Hare International   6

    CHAPTER 3 – Fort Collins; Silver Grille Cafe   8

October 26

    CHAPTER 4 – Loveland, Colorado   11

October 27

    CHAPTER 5 – Lokoma Village   12

October 28

    CHAPTER 6 – Niwot, Colorado   14

    CHAPTER 7 – Peggy's Cove, Nova Scotia   21

October 29

    CHAPTER 8 – Lokoma Village   25

    CHAPTER 9 – Rome: Da Vinci Airport   28

October 30

    CHAPTER 10 – Lokoma Village   30

    CHAPTER 11 – Lokoma Village   32

    CHAPTER 12 – Cameron Pass   34

    CHAPTER 13 – Lokoma Village   36

November 2

    CHAPTER 14 - Liv's Journal   38

November 4

    CHAPTER 15 – Fort Collins High   40

November 5

    CHAPTER 16 – Lokoma Village   45

    CHAPTER 17 – Prodeus Headquarters   48

November 6

    CHAPTER 18 – Clement Home   50

November 12

    CHAPTER 19 – Freetown: Refugee Village   52

November 13

    CHAPTER 20 – Liv's Diary   59

November 14

    CHAPTER 21 – Prodeus Headquarters   60

    CHAPTER 22 – Fort Collins High School   63

    CHAPTER 23 – Poudre Valley Hospital   67

November 17

    CHAPTER 24 – Rebel Camp   71

November 18

    CHAPTER 25 – Fort Collins High   74

    CHAPTER 26 – Prodeus Headquarters   77

November 19

    CHAPTER 27 – Clement Home   82

November 20

    CHAPTER 28 – Prodeus Boardroom   84

    CHAPTER 29 – Jennifer's Apartment   88

November 21

    CHAPTER 30 – Café outside the Vatican   89

November 22

    CHAPTER 31 – Rawah Wilderness   94

    CHAPTER 32 – Shadyside, Pennsylvania   98

November 24

    CHAPTER 33 – Silver Grill Café   100

    CHAPTER 34 – Loveland Colorado   104

    CHAPTER 35 – Walden, Colorado   105

    CHAPTER 36 – Thatcher Estate: Virginia   108

About the Author   Appendix.... Page 2

Character Summaries   Appendix.... Page 3

Summary of Birthright: Public Offerings Book One

In a secret lab high up in Cameron Pass in the Colorado Rockies, Sheila Stratemeier, a drug developer for the Aldrich Institute, believes the Aldrich no longer focuses on a mission to save lives. She knows now that the Institute's executives do not plan to use their new malaria vaccine to cure people – at least not in the short term. Instead, they plan to first cull the population in a twisted eugenics plot that will kill as many as a million. As she prepares to blow the whistle on her company, Sheila is killed at her desk

Dave Clement works covertly with Sheila to identify a cure for his daughter's drug resistant HIV. While Dave is passionate about his work, finding a cure for his daughter tops his priority list. Five weeks before Sheila's demise, Dave travels on a business trip to Nigeria and then Sierra Leone in West Africa. He is the Vice President of Operations and Business Development for Prodeus, a partner of the Aldrich Institute where Sheila works. Prodeus makes a Portable DNA Analyzer (PDNA) that can quickly test an individual's blood and DNA to ascertain if they have the genetic make-up to benefit from the new malaria vaccine developed by Sheila's team at the Aldrich. To fund a pilot program for the vaccine and deployment of his PDNAs in Sierra Leone, Dave works closely with Evan Conger, the World Health Organization Assistant Director-General for HIV/AIDS and Malaria, and Adrian Guerra, the West African Country Director for the World Bank. They recruit the Lokoma tribe of northwestern Sierra Leone to be the first recipients of the new vaccine in the pilot program. All of Sierra Leone still suffers in the aftermath of the Ebola pandemic; the economy is devastated and its people struggle with high malnutrition levels, making them more vulnerable to death from malaria, the biggest single killer of children. Hamara Karanja, the tribe's chief, has lost one daughter to malaria already and wants to protect his two remaining children, Jacob and Emma. Hamara works closely with Father Jim Reilly, an Irish missionary priest who brings anti-malarial drugs and outside medical missions to Lokoma village. Father Jim first introduced Hamara to Dave Clement years earlier as part of a medical mission to the village. The long-term relationship between Father Jim, Dave and Hamara is the connection that results in the final decision to move the malaria vaccine pilot program from Nigeria, beset by the Boko Haram, to Sierra Leone, starting with the Lokoma tribe.

At home in Fort Collins, Colorado, Dave's daughter struggles with illusions induced by medication she is taking to manage her HIV. At 15, Liv Clement has allegedly engaged in no risky behaviors to cause her to become infected with AIDS. Liv's HIV is a secret only her immediate family, doctors and Sheila know. Dave suspects that Liv must have had some intimate encounter that led to her infection. As a result of that suspicion and his preoccupation with work over family, Mel Clement, Dave's wife, throws him out of the house. They are now separated. Liv, in particular, struggles with the family situation as she copes with her secret disease and with HIV drugs to which her disease quickly builds resistance. She fears she is facing a death sentence. Because of the nature of HIV, Liv keeps it from even her closest friends who she fears will shame her.

Claire McQuaid is executive director of the Aldrich Institute. She has extensive scarring on her body from an unspecified incident in her youth. The scarring and the unspecified incident that caused it preoccupy her and somehow help her focus on her mission to eradicate malaria. She seems obsessed with terror attacks and genocides, occasionally watching a video compilation on her computer to remind herself of the horrors.

Jennifer Winter once worked alongside Sheila Stratemeier when both were protégés of Claire at the Aldrich. When Claire helped Ed Hepp set up Prodeus to manufacture PDNAs to enable optimized delivery of the malaria vaccine, Claire arranged for Jennifer to go to work at Prodeus as project manager for the PDNA development. Jennifer works directly for Dave Clement. She is up to something with Dave, seeming to encourage his separation from Mel and making a play for him to be her lover. Dave rebuffs her advances, insisting he is happily married and that he will put things back together with Mel.

When Dave does have a chance to get back with Mel by joining her at Liv's volleyball game, he gets delayed by a meeting with Jennifer and Brian Middleton, the Prodeus VP of Engineering. He shows up late to the game, but Mel and Liv join him for dinner afterward. There, he tells them the good news that his quest for a cure for Liv is finally bearing fruit. Through their covert cloud account, Sheila has told him she has found a path to a cure. Sheila plans to meet with him in person the following week to give him the details. Unfortunately, Dave needs to leave dinner early to catch a flight. He has agreed to meet Evan Conger at the Admirals Club at the Denver International Airport before boarding. Evan needs to tell him about something that affects the malaria project and Liv. Both men are on the same flight to Geneva and the WHO conference there. Dave's early departure from dinner reinforces his family's feeling that work is more important to Dave than they are. Mel is angry with him. Liv is very hurt; she misses her Dad and wants her parents to get back together. At the same time, they want him to learn more about Sheila's discovery.

The Geneva flight has trouble over Nova Scotia and smoke pours into the cabin. On Evan's visit to the Aldrich lab in Denver, Sheila slipped him a flash drive with information that shows that Claire McQuaid and the Aldrich are willing to risk genocide in West Africa as part of their deployment of the malaria vaccine. It's part of complicated chemistry that hides proteins that will cause an HIV mutation inside the vaccine. Anyone with HIV who receives the vaccine will get the mutation. The mutation is much more deadly than the regular strain of HIV in Sierra Leone. It kills in months instead of a decade and there are no drugs that can stop it. The Aldrich, however, has a way of eradicating the mutation once antibodies are collected from its victims. But while the Aldrich waits to collect antibodies, those with the mutation will drop by the tens of thousands, potentially up to a million losing their lives before the Aldrich is able to use the antibodies to deploy the HIV vaccine that will stop it.

Evan, sitting in business class on the Geneva flight, thinks of Dave in the coach section of the plane. He had hoped Dave and he would stop the Aldrich plot, but now he realizes the plane is not going to stay in the air. He also now knows that the plot specifically endangers Dave's daughter. He quickly types a note into his phone, secure in a waterproof and shockproof case, to try to find a way to get Sheila's information to someone else. The plane crashes into the Atlantic, with everyone on board presumed dead.

In Fort Collins, Mel Clement sees the news of the plane crash on CNN. She realizes it's Dave's flight and immediately leaves a message on his mobile phone, telling him that she wants him back home and that she loves him. Hearing the news that the crash has no survivors, Mel breaks down in sobs.

At the Aldrich Mountain Lab, Eldridge Perry, head of drug development and Sheila's boss, speaks with Claire on the phone. He realizes that Claire's security force has somehow arranged for the Geneva-bound plane to go down. He is not happy with the thuggish tactics of the IRA-trained security chief, but does not argue with Claire, recognizing that the mission of the Aldrich is bigger than all of them. He thinks about the chess pieces the Aldrich yet has available to ensure successful implementation of the plan in West Africa. He focuses on Liv Clement, recognizing that she is a key pawn in keeping the plan on course, all because she is Dave's daughter. Thinking about Liv and the threat to her, Eldridge mumbles aloud: "Helluva birthright."

As Book 2 begins, Dave's plane has crashed with all aboard lost, Evan Conger is dead, and Sheila has lost her outside relationships that could stop the Aldrich's genocidal plan. While Sheila apparently has some way to bring help to Liv Clement for her HIV, the crash of the Geneva-bound plane and Eldridge Perry's targeting of Liv Clement as a doomed pawn in the Aldrich conspiracy change everything, promising deadly trouble ahead for Sheila, Liv and the people of Lokoma Village.

PUBLIC OFFERINGS

BOOK TWO

The Price of a Life

CHAPTER 1

Southeastern Sierra Leone, Kono District
October 22, 10:15 am GMT

His stethoscope hung around his neck as a matter of habit, offering the only visible clue that Warren Sturbridge, close friend and protégé of Evan Conger, practiced medicine. He walked up the narrow path, thick grass over six feet tall brushing at his sides, his twenty-something companion a half-step behind. After five months in Sierra Leone, Sturbridge learned from the locals to walk at a much easier pace than he did when he first arrived from San Diego. The soaking humidity and tropical sun ensured he remembered the lesson.

"When your laptop disappeared, I thought we would never get the report finished," said Tom Czerski, a short but lean man now, just over a year into his two-year Peace Corps tour.

"I told you to have faith," said Sturbridge, a week's worth of gray and black stubble on his face. "Pen and paper may be slow, but it's very reliable."

The men walked carefully around a small bomb crater in the trail, knowing that craters provided excellent cover for booby traps. While peace had been officially declared, the real experience on the ground, particularly outside the main cities, displayed a balkanized array of competing militias and stragglers who knew only violence as a means to achieve their ends. Booby traps, landmines, checkpoints, ambush, and intimidation remained the norm in the bush.

Sturbridge had arrived in the country with a decent paunch on his belt. That had been gone for months and his legs, arms and abs had begun to show definition that he looked forward to proudly showing off to his wife upon his return home. He viewed the overall experience as very invigorating but missed his wife and his two-year-old son – and hot showers.

"The World Bank guy – Adrian Guerra – must think you have a good chance of getting the funds," Czerski said.

"Why? Because Adrian volunteered his office to type the report?" Sturbridge replied.

"Do you think he'd waste his time?"

"No. No, I guess not. Something about the guy just sets off my alarm bells." Hearing movement in the tall grass, the doctor held a hand up and both men stopped, holding their breath as they listened.

"What is it?" Czerski asked.

"Bird probably," the doctor responded as he wiped his already damp shirt against the side of his face to stop the trickle of an irritating drop of sweat. He listened for further sounds but heard nothing else out of the ordinary. After thirty seconds, he nodded at the volunteer and they continued walking.

"Will Adrian or his World Bank team e-mail a copy of the finished product back to the Salk Institute?" Czerski asked.

"Not until I proofread it," Sturbridge said. "The copy I asked them to type is a photocopy of the handwritten version I faxed to Dr. Conger a few days ago. Evan knows me well enough that I don't mind him catching a few grammatical errors. The important thing is that we've identified the HIV type here."

Thunder rumbled in the distance, a common rainy season event. The season would be over in a few months, but Sturbridge would be gone by then, so he might never know Sierra Leone without rain and mud.

"Will people be surprised that it's the same type as there is throughout the rest of the region?" Czerski quizzed, his breath starting to catch as the trail inclined upward steeply.

"Some will be. There are a few scientists that want new mutations to show up because they believe new variations could be more aggressive with shorter incubation periods. Shorter incubation periods could offer new pathways to cures and vaccines."

"Do you agree?" the Peace Corps volunteer asked.

"No. It's wishful thinking. The consistency we've discovered is good news. A little bit of stability gives us a better shot at beating this damned scourge. At least for a while."

"From the conversation I overheard with you and Adrian, he's definitely not in your camp on that."

"No, he's not."

The air turned green as the sun went behind the first of the rapidly advancing thunderheads. Sturbridge could almost taste the rain.

He had rushed the handwritten copy of his research in hopes that Evan Conger would present the key findings at the WHO conference that week. Adrian Guerra wanted to believe that Sierra Leone and other areas of West Africa had a different and more aggressive HIV type. Sturbridge concluded that was not the case, but Guerra stubbornly and inexplicably insisted the doctor was wrong.

Big drops of rain began falling and lightning struck with a crackling roar nearby.

"Doctor!" A voice called to Sturbridge and Czerski through sheets of rain that suddenly began blowing across their path. They hurried up the trail, arriving quickly at a large clearing.

"Doctor! Over here."

They entered the clearing and saw the man standing 30 yards off the path to the right. Sturbridge recognized him as one of the Leonean clerks from Adrian Guerra's World Bank office.

"What are you doing out here?" the doctor shouted over the rain.

The man waved a pile of paper at the men. "You know what this is?" the clerk called.

Sturbridge stopped in his tracks. It looked like his handwritten report. And it was getting drenched. "Is that my report?" he demanded.

"Yes, it is," the man yelled, an insane grin on his face.

"Why are you here with it? Is it finished? Have you typed it?"

"No, doctor. It's not finished. You must come see it."

Sturbridge looked at Czerski. The men shared a look that said, "What the hell…"

"Thank God you faxed one to Dr. Conger," Czerski said.

"We're going to get the original back right now," the doctor said.

With Sturbridge in the lead, they veered off the path and ran across the soppy clearing toward the clerk. As they closed the gap to about 15 yards, the clerk turned and raced into the brush behind him.

"Where are you going?" shouted the doctor. No good could come of this, he thought. He chastised himself for trusting Guerra.

They picked up their pace, the doctor staying just ahead of Czerski. Sturbridge felt the slight tension of the wire against his shin as it snapped from his momentum. He had cared for many victims of similar booby traps over the preceding months. He knew the odds. He turned wide-eyed to his young protégé whose wet face mirrored the terror on his own just before the bright, white flash of the explosion.

CHAPTER 2

Chicago - O'Hare Airport Admiral's Club
October 22 - 5:02 am Central Time

Drawn by the addictive aroma of fresh coffee, a bleary-eyed Dave Clement pushed the espresso machine's cappuccino button. As he watched the foamy liquid fill his cup, he wondered if the energy from the caffeine would trump the sleepiness the milky forth could induce. While he waited for the pour to finish, he straightened his shirt collar and smoothed the seam in his slacks. His clothes had not held up well during a long, restless night in a lounge chair in the Admirals Club. He could barely walk, let alone think.

He looked at the wall clock. 5:02 a.m. He had only a few minutes until he needed to go to the concourse for his flight to New York. Once in the Big Apple, he would take a cab from LaGuardia to JFK and catch a flight to Paris. From there, he would finally connect to Geneva on Air France. He would arrive in Switzerland at 8:30 in the morning, two days separated from a bed, a good night's sleep and a shower. Definitely an ordeal, but he would end up missing only the conference's opening cocktail reception. He hoped he would catch enough sleep en route to keep him awake for the meetings and sessions which he would start as soon as he arrived from the airport. Damned security line at DIA had been backed up at 7:40 the night before. Even with the long line, he would have been on time if TSA had not randomly pulled him out of line for a selective hand check. For some unexplained reason, they singled him out. First time in a decade for him. Only God knows why, he thought.

Once clear of the checkpoint, he flew down the escalator and caught a train right away. Five more minutes and he would have been on the flight to London and talking with Evan. Five more minutes would have saved him twelve hours of extra travel time. Instead, he spent the next hour finding new flights that would get him to Geneva as closely as possible to his missed connection. That put him on United to Chicago, connecting to American.

Four flights instead of two. On the bright side, it was good for extra frequent flyer segments to maintain his elite status. Nonetheless, the torture started immediately with a middle seat against the bathrooms in the back of coach flying out of Denver; the armrests seemed narrower than his hips. He had not been able to get international business class out of Chicago, but at least he had an aisle and American had some legroom in coach, especially on the triple seven.

When he arrived in Chicago, he reached for his phone to call Mel. Just like he always did when he traveled. The phone's LED readout told him it was 11:50 in Chicago, making it 10:50 in Fort Collins. Too late to call Mel without waking her. He had already pushed his luck with her earlier in the day. If he woke her, it would be a backward move, not a forward one. Instead, he called her mobile phone, figuring it would be turned off as per her habit, reposing in its charger for the night.

"Hi, Mel," he said to her voice mail. "Just wanted to tell you how great it was to be with you and Liv again. I know I rushed out tonight, but I hope you know my intentions were good..."

She won't buy that, he thought. He tried again. "I'm in Chicago. Trying to sleep on a chair in the Admirals Club. Missed my flight out of Denver so I have kind of an ordeal now to make my meeting in Geneva tomorrow. Spending time with you was definitely worth it. The people in Geneva will just have to understand that there's nothing more important than my family. I love you. Very much. With all my heart. Tell Liv the same, please. Bye. Love you. Love you both."

He pressed a button. That sounds manipulative, he thought. Very manipulative. He went through the prompts and canceled the message.

Shoving the phone back in his jacket pocket, he pondered taking an early morning flight back to Denver. With the time difference, he could be there by 8:30 in the morning. Not a good idea, he thought. Not yet. An hour later, the pings from texts with flight status woke him up as he finally dozed off. Irritated and groggy, he powered off his phone and nodded off again,

Now, five hours later, he finished his cappuccino and reached down for the handle on his rolling bag. With his free hand, he pulled his phone out of his pocket, discovering it was still turned off. He powered it on and headed for his plane. Waiting for the elevator to the concourse, he saw he had a voicemail from Mel. As he pressed the button to hear it, he glimpsed Fox News on a monitor to the left of the elevators. He picked up the words "airline disaster" on the marquis running along the bottom of the screen. He stepped toward the television, looking for a volume control.

"Can I help you, sir?" called a woman behind the reception desk.

"I can't hear it."

She aimed a remote past Dave, but the station cut to commercial.

"It said airline disaster," he said. "Do you know what happened?"

The voicemail started its playback in his ear: "Dave, I don't care what time you get this. Please call me. I need to know you're okay. I love you. I'm so sorry for everything."

"Doesn't look good," the receptionist answered. "Flight went down off Nova Scotia."

Dave glanced at the list of voicemails on his phone. Six more from Mel, the last only twenty minutes earlier. "Canadian flight?" he asked the receptionist.

"Flight out of Denver bound for London," she said.

The handle of the rolling bag slipped out of Dave's fingers, banging off the floor.

CHAPTER 3

Fort Collins, Colorado; Silver Grille Cafe
October 22, 9:55 a.m. Mountain Time

Five hours later, Dave sat with Mel in a booth at the Silver Grille Café in downtown Fort Collins. He ordered eggs over easy and corned beef hash with a side of cinnamon toast, buttered and grilled slices of the restaurant's enormous cinnamon buns whose sweet and spicy aroma permeated the dining area. For once, Mel did not challenge him for ordering too much.

He sipped his coffee and adjusted his cup back in the saucer. Mel reached around it to take his hand in hers.

"I love you," she said.

"I love you, too. More than ever. I'm blessed to have you in my life."

Mel tilted her head and narrowed her eyes. He knew she was not accustomed to that kind of language from him.

"God spared me, Mel," he said.

"I'll say. God and the fact that the TSA pulled you out of the security line."

"For sure. If they don't do that, I'm on that flight. First time I've been pulled out in a decade probably. What are the odds? That's the good Lord looking out for me."

Mel nodded and squeezed his hand in both of hers. "It's time you came home."

He felt tears well up in his eyes. He had waited months for her to say that. He looked toward the wall and tried to wipe away the first traces with his fingers, but the feeling was too strong and a handful of tears made it over his cheeks and down to his jawline.

"I'm sorry," he mumbled.

"For tears?" she asked, her own tears now glistening below her eyes. "Don't be silly. If we can't cry a little about this, we don't, ah, we don't…"

She sobbed once and then inhaled deeply to stop herself from continuing.

He wanted desperately to go home with her. But he had deliberately asked her to meet him here first for breakfast after she dropped Liv at school. He knew if he drove directly home from the airport, he would find it almost impossible to do what he was about to do. He took both her hands now and looked directly into her eyes.

"I want to move back home more than anything. I know that I've made you and Liv secondary to my work. It's been misguided. I want to do better."

"It's okay. I understand. You obsess with your work because you worry about taking care of us. I know that. Before Liv came along and we had responsibilities, you knew how to relax. I just want that Dave back, the one I married."

"That Dave may never come back," he said. "In the moments after I saw the news about the plane, when I realized that Evan and his team were gone, something came to me. Something very insistent. And I can't let it go. I'm called to see this through in the business, to be more focused than ever. It's what I'm meant to do."

Mel let go of his hands and sat back, her mouth slightly agape. "I don't understand," she said.

"If I come home now, I won't be what I need to be at home. I'll disappoint you again."

"What?"

"I've been spared for a reason."

"Omigod, Dave. Don't do this."

"I'm serious. God wants me to have faith and double down on the vaccine effort. I don't know why, but I think it has something to do with finding a cure for Liv."

Mel's eyes blazed. "So you're not coming home? You're going to get on more airplanes? You're going to leave us to worry about you?"

"At least for a few weeks. I need to focus on the vaccine project. And I don't want to bring home the same workaholic problem that caused you to lock me out in the first place."

She leaned back in her seat and studied him. "You're not looking at this the right way, Dave. You've been spared to come home and be with us. Not to run around the world trying to be a hero."

"I only wish that's all it was."

"What the hell is wrong with you?"

"It's bigger than me."

"Bigger than us?"

He bit the inside of his cheek thoughtfully before answering. "I think so."

"So you're the damned second-coming now? It wasn't enough to think you were the savior of this family. You have to save the world. You need psychiatric help."

It surprised Dave that he remained peaceful both inside and out. "I truly love you, Mel. And I love Liv. More than anything in this world."

"Then come home. You're not the only one who got a second chance. We all did."

"I'd like nothing more, but it's too soon. You wouldn't be happy with me. For a while, I'm going to be gone more than ever, working harder than ever. Sorting out…"

"Why God spared you," she said, finishing for him. "And because you're big-time Dave Clement, the reason has to be earth-shaking. World class, right?"

"You don't believe me? You think it was just random that I missed that plane?"

Mel covered her eyes with her hands. She took a few deep breaths, working on perspective. "Listen, my love…"

When Mel said "my love" to him, she always meant it in the most condescending sense.

"…even if you did benefit from some cosmic intervention. I'd like to think that God appreciates the simple things, too – that His intervention isn't just reserved for world issues. And, if it is in this case, maybe it's about being home for your daughter, helping her grow up to be President or some other thing that meets your ego requirements."

He reached for her hands again, but she folded her arms in response.

"You are the most wonderful gift God ever gave me," he said. "I don't consider that a simple thing, but it's not a world issue. God does care about the day-to-day things. You're absolutely right. Fortunately or unfortunately, I know he wants me to do something that does not seem to fit our family plan. That knowledge is deep inside me, right at the core. For once, I need to be obedient."

She wiped the back of a hand across her eyes, her make-up streaked and eyes black from mascara. She tried again. "What about Liv's health? She needs an involved father."

"I think that's part of what I'll be doing. Conger was very involved in HIV management."

"That's not the same thing as being at home for her. She needs you to be a father first, not a champion."

He could feel a slight tear in the fabric of his resolve. He knew, though, that if he went home, he would quickly lose sight of the big picture and be drawn right back into the place where he most wanted to be.

Mel stared through him, shaking her head. Then she carefully folded her white cloth napkin and laid it on the table. She stood up. "You're breaking your daughter's heart."

"I'm trying to protect her."

Mel turned and walked away. He did not follow. He knew there was no point. He had let her down again. The clever idea of not yet going home seemed a lot less appealing than it did in the middle of the night at O'Hare International. He picked up the coffee cup and brought it to his lips, but did not drink. He put it back down and just stared into the black liquid.

"What the hell am I doing?" he mumbled.

CHAPTER 4

Loveland, Colorado: Prodeus Offices
October 26, 2:58 a.m. Mountain Time

Her facial features shrouded in shadows from the computer screen's blue light, Jennifer maneuvered her mouse in the darkness. To avoid discovery, she relied only on the screen's reflected light. The digital clock in the lower right hand corner of the screen said 2:58 a.m.

With the mouse, she pointed the arrow on the screen at "insert." A click sounded and a menu with more options dropped down. She slid the arrow to "files." A directory of file names blossomed on to the screen.

Leaning forward in her chair, she studied the names. She glanced at the paper on her desk that listed the confidential files she needed, files only accessible through secure computers in the office. One by one, she selected them. Small boxes representing copies of the files immediately appeared in the e-mail Jennifer prepared.

Closing the file directory, she rose from her seat and walked out of the cubicle into the darkness. She looked toward the windows that looked to the moonlit mountains. She listened for a moment. A fan from a heating unit rumbled in the distance. Nothing out of the ordinary.

Back in the cube, Jennifer opened her purse and pulled out a CD that she never let out of her possession. She knew never to leave it at the office. She put it on the tray in her desktop computer, reminding herself to make sure to remove it again when she finished. She waited while a program automatically started. She counted backward from 100 to make the time go faster. A moment later, a screen popped up asking for a password. In the low blue light, she keyed in an eight digit alphanumeric combination and clicked "OK" twice in succession. She sat back in her chair and waited.

The CD tray hummed as the computer read instructions from the disc. In less than a minute, a box appeared in the middle of the computer screen. "Encryption completed," it declared.

Jennifer clicked *send* on the e-mail with all the attachments. When the computer showed the package successfully transmitted, Jennifer opened her "sent items" folder and deleted her computer's copy of the e-mail.

She heard a loud clicking sound from across the building. She did not know if it was a person or creaking vents. She stood and peered over the cubicle looking for signs of movement. Quickly snapping her briefcase shut, she listened for further sounds, but only heard the whirring of the CD in its tray. She walked out of her cubicle, careful not to trip in the darkness, still listening for more noises. As she traveled further away from her cube, the whirring of the very sensitive CD she left behind grew fainter and finally stopped.

CHAPTER 5

Lokoma Village
October 27 - 3 am GMT

The croaking of frogs and cicadas faded. The muggy night grew silent. Hamara heard his breath passing slowly in and out through his nose. The musty smell of mold and decay mingled with the perfumed fragrance of new blossoms. Shifting his position on the smooth rock that acted as his seat, he listened to the first weak twitter of waking birds as the black of night paled to gray. Then, the first misty rays of morning sun passed through the narrow gaps in the thick jungle canopy, waking dozens of avian species whose songs sprang to life in a swelling cacophony.

He bounced a river pebble in his hand. The devil resided in this pebble – or so he was taught as a boy. Maboru, the magic in which he trained as both chief and diviner, taught that the pebble had great powers. It taught, for example, that a pebble could judge a man in a capital case. If it sank to the bottom of a bucket of water, it condemned the accused to a death sentence; if it floated, it freed him.

He could not imagine the dense pebble floating under any circumstances.

He wished that it did have magical powers. He would use it to make Sara well, to protect Jacob, to shield his village from sickness and violence. But if his experience as chief had taught him nothing else, it taught him that Maboru amounted to a centuries old scam. Somewhere along the way, people used it to gain favor with others, persuading the simple-minded of some magic to which only the diviner held the secret. Hamara now knew that magic amounted to nothing more than a mix of salesmanship, science and coincidence – and sometimes luck. The diviners, or witch doctors as whites once called them, played to the fears of uneducated, hardworking people who had never been more than a few miles from their birthplace. These people, their progeny and their ancestors lived in terror for centuries. First Islamic traders from the northeast and then local chieftains in league with the Europeans tracked them down, chaining and caging them like animals, ripping them away from everything they held dear.

With the healthiest and most attractive often the first to go, the tribes often experienced something akin to natural selection in reverse. Ultimately, their most beautiful young women found themselves among the many wives of the Islamic slave traders. The sturdiest women ended up chained inside the stinking holds of slave ships with the sturdiest young men; together they brought top dollar as laborers for distant plantations in the Americas.

The stories passed down to Hamara said that 30% of them died en route, disease rampant as they wallowed in one another's fluids and waste in the dark holds of the pitching ships.

Rolling the pebble between thumb and fingers, he scanned the trees and the red earth beneath them. How many times had his ancestors moved until they found this remote place? How far had they run from the sins of slavery? For five generations, the Lokoma tilled this very soil, mined its bauxite, conceived children on it and buried their dead in it. The magic of invisibility, not river pebbles or cowry shells, kept the Lokoma safe. The land and its location protected them. And they thrived through contentment with the blessings surrounding them in the rainforest. No promise of greater earthly riches tempted the Lokoma from their malaria-infested version of paradise.

Now white men had once more discovered them, just as they had in the time of the slave trade. Now, they came to bring a cure for malaria. But history taught that these do-gooders also brought other, as yet unclear, agendas.

But mostly, Hamara ached that the alleged cure came four months too late for seven-year-old Ketta. The heartache doubled him over as he remembered holding her tiny body in his arms, again felt her warm breath on his neck; she whispered "Pa" before growing still. He did not let her go until the heat of her fever faded to cold, his own tears coating her cheeks as he gently laid her back on her mat.

Earlier this night, as he left the hut in the darkness, he softly touched Sara's forehead with the back of his hand. Sleep had again eased her fever. The Americans' magic vaccine would not get here soon enough for her. She would either pull through or not. Fr. Jim did not show up as promised. Adrian Guerra had come instead. Fr. Jim had never before let him down.

Mariama said she dreamed that a spell made the malaria stronger than Sara's quinine tabs. Rumors had spread throughout the mountains that just such a spell had been cast over villages that refused to convert to the ways of Allah. Fr. Jim had assured her that the power of Jesus Christ would fight off any devil's spells, but he did not guarantee that the magic of Christ would make Sara well. It had not cured Ketta; her last Eucharist still digesting in her stomach when she expired. No, unlike the gods of the jungle and unlike the devils who falsely claimed to speak for Allah, Fr. Jim's God made no promises about miracles in this life.

That touch of honesty had caused Hamara to lead the Lokoma to conversion to the priest's religion. Hamara trusted Fr. Jim, relied on him. And Fr. Jim had brought Dave Clement and his family. They gave without taking because they were followers of the priest's God. Now Hamara prayed he had not been naïve about the American, that all of the generosity had not just been a long-term setup to use his people for personal gain.

He turned his hand palm down, the pebble dropping to the ground with an almost imperceptible thump. Falling to his knees, he made certain to face east. Bending forward, he prayed for the well-being of his family and of his people – and for time.

CHAPTER 6

Niwot, Colorado; Evan Conger's Memorial Service
October 28, 10:40 a.m. Mountain Time

Sheila Stratemeier pulled her overcoat tighter against the downslope winds that whipped over the eastern slope of Colorado's Rockies and across the St. Vrain Valley, charging up the hills over the village of Niwot. Atop one of those hills, she and nearly three hundred others stood on an undeveloped two-acre lot that had represented one of Evan Conger's fondest dreams. There, in the face of the chilling downslope bluster, underneath a roiling overcast sky, Sheila gathered with Evan Conger's friends and family to memorialize him this noon on the grassy crest of the hill. They stood in a large circle around a portrait of Evan draped in black and surrounded by fresh-cut flowers.

Evan's brother-in-law, a Lutheran pastor from Evan's hometown of Sioux City, Iowa, read Bible verses selected by Evan's wife, each meant to touch on some aspect of Evan that she sought to honor or simply remember this day. No choir sang. Sheila remembered that Michelle Conger knew her husband liked nothing better than the song of nature atop this hill facing the silver-white peaks of the Rockies. Here, she heard they planned to build their retirement home. The story that spread in the lab said that here, under the stars, often cuddled in a blanket with the top down on their red Thunderbird, Michelle and Evan listened to the hoot of owls, the songs of birds, and the howl of a coyote on a moonlit night. On some nights, the story went, great balls of tumbleweed bounced by them on the wind. Inevitably, Evan would break into a brief rendition of "Tumblin' Tumbleweeds," completely corny and entirely orthogonal to his public image. Sheila saw Michelle smile and wondered if she was thinking of it now.

"Evan led his life with complete regard for others," declared the pastor into a microphone to overcome the noise of the wind. "I knew him for over 35 years, since he first dated my sister, his wife. He championed DNA analysis as part of his research efforts at the Aldrich Institute. Someday, when the science matures a bit more, someone will study his DNA. It will show he did not have a single selfish gene. Here was a man who could have no enemies…"

Sheila shifted uneasily on her heels. She stared unconsciously at Claire McQuaid until Claire caught her looking. Sheila quickly looked away. In her peripheral vision, Sheila saw Claire's green eyes flash and her nose flare. A few people to her left, Sheila saw her one-time best friend Jennifer Winter, focused intently on the pastor's words. Always the dedicated follower, thought Sheila. For nearly a week now, since Conger's death, Jennifer had ignored Sheila's emails asking for help with Claire and Eldridge. Sheila did not know what form that help needed to take; she only knew that she could no longer handle it alone. And time was running out to de-rail this train.

Near the far corner of the podium, she recognized Dave Clement. It surprised her to see him without his wife. Mel inevitably accompanied Dave to events. Her absence presented an opportunity for Sheila to speak to him alone. Youssef Khalfani, the UN Secretary General, stood beside Dave. Occasionally, Khalfani and Dave exchanged whispered comments. The two men had first come to know each other during the Ebola pandemic and now belonged to a small circle that centered around Evan in the quest to conquer tropical disease. With Conger gone, she needed to get to Dave. He could help her. And he needed to know what she knew about his daughter.

In her brief comments, Michelle Conger said that her husband had passed through just like the wind, but, just like the wind, he would keep coming back, ever churning in their hearts. She said that if and when they did find his body, it would not be him because, through the grace of an almighty and loving God, he had already come home.

"Feel the wind," she said. "Feel his presence. He is here with us now as he will always be."

Sheila wondered if she could be as hopeful as Michelle if it been her life partner taken in some inexplicable random selection. She prayed that Evan could actually be there. She prayed that his soul might intervene with God to bring her help. Urgently.

When Conger's service ended, the mourners lined up to hug Michelle and her two grown children. Sheila approached Dave Clement as he broke from the line.

"Hi, Dave." She touched the shoulder of his blue cashmere overcoat.

Dave turned. "Sheila. Hello."

"We need to talk. Alone."

"Sure."

Her eyes scanned the people nearby. She started walking, steering him away from the crowd. The wind would cover their conversation for anyone not right on top of them. "Sorry we couldn't meet this morning," she said, leaning up to his face on her toes, her words barely discernible in the howling wind.

He leaned down toward her. "I understand. We'll reset.".

"I don't know when," she said, "Security's getting tighter. They're watching me."

Dave leaned closer, struggling to hear her. "Who?" he asked. "Who's watching you?"

"The IRA thugs." She nodded in the direction of several men in large black overcoats.

"Can you send details to the cloud?"

Sheila held her Denver Broncos stocking cap on with one hand as it threatened to blow off. "That's just the point. I went in last night and found my access blocked. The Aldrich has blacklisted the cloud URL."

Dave's eyes widened. "So they must know. Can you use another one?"

She leaned close to his ear. "Won't make any difference. They know what to look for now."

"Will you be all right?"

"I'll be fine. But you need to know about Liv. Everything's not what it seems - "

A hand landed on Sheila's shoulder. She turned to see Mike Farley, the Aldrich head of security. She shook him off and turned back to Dave. She pulled out a business card from her coat pocket.

"Claire's ready to go," Farley said. "She and Mr. Clement have a lunch scheduled."

"I just wanted to introduce myself to our most important partner," Sheila said, handing Dave the card.

"I need another minute here," Dave said.

"Ten seconds, sir," Farley said, an Irish brogue apparent in a trilled 'r'. Then he stood there, hands folded in front of him.

"Alone," Dave said.

Farley looked back and forth at the two and then at his watch. "We need to go now," he said. He tugged at Dave's arm. Dave pulled back.

"It's okay, Dave," Sheila said. "We can talk again. Can't keep Claire waiting."

The security chief escorted Dave to McQuaid's limo. Dave looked back at Sheila. She nodded assurance.

"What did she want?" Farley asked as he squeezed Dave's arm a little too tightly.

"An introduction."

"Anything else?" he asked.

"You didn't give her time for anything else."

"Wait here," Farley said as he reached the back door of the limo. He leaned in and spoke inaudibly to McQuaid. He stepped back and Dave slid into the backseat.

From the back of the limo, Claire watched her security chief corral Dave. She did not want to add Sheila as a variable in managing the Prodeus exec. His relationships and ability to pull off the malaria project mattered more than ever with Evan gone.

"Strange place to network," she said to him as he entered the limo. As she spoke, she watched the retreating Sheila through the car's tinted window.

"I don't understand," Dave said.

"She's a good scientist, but we think she's getting a little claustrophobic in the mountain lab. Might be looking to make a change."

"Claire, I'd never pilfer one of your people -"

"I know that. Unfortunately, others might, and we can't afford to lose her."

"Pretty critical skills?"

"That. And she knows too many of our secrets." Claire looked down at her carefully manicured nails. Physical perfection had been beyond her reach for years. Mourning a death reassured her that the physical mattered little. Her nails reminded her that she could pull it off for a little while. Uninvited, fire flashed into her mind. Shouts and screams.

"Can you imagine the horror?" Claire asked. "A lot of them died from smoke inhalation. A blessing, I suppose. Passing out. But many of them burned alive. Wide awake when the flames reached them…" Her hands trembled. "My God, Dave. Where do you run in a slowly burning airplane? The engine, the shell just kept flying while the plastic inside melted."

He reached out his hand. She gently waved him off and then dabbed a tissue under each eye, careful not to smear her make-up.

"I don't think Michelle really wants to find his body," she said. "Or what's left of it." She leaned forward and opened the limo's refrigerator. "Want a drink?"

"No," Dave answered. "No, thank you."

She found diet tonic water. Carbonation hissed as she pulled back the tab. "So, Evan's misfortune has left us a mess to sort out with W-H-O," she said as she moved the can to her lips.

Boulder, Colorado; Boulder Café
October 28 - 11:45 a.m. Mountain Time

In the face of blowing snow, Claire latched on to Dave's arm as her three-inch heels gingerly navigated the irregular cobblestones of the Pearl Street Mall. On the short walk from the curb to the granite entryway of the Boulder Cafe, wind whipped down the cavernous outdoor mall cutting through them like a thousand tiny icicles. Dave hunched forward into the frigid blast, regretting that he left his overcoat in the limo.

They entered the restaurant, stomping snow off their feet on a large red mat. The hostess, an anorexic-looking young woman with a small silver ball on the tip of her tongue and countless earrings, recognized Claire immediately.

"Good afternoon, Ms. McQuaid. We have your table ready."

They followed the hostess to a distant corner booth with high padded wooden backs suitable for privacy. Scooting across the bench to the window, Dave felt a twenty degree drop in temperature at the sill where nearly two inches of snow had already piled up on the outside ledge.

"Your trip home's going to be treacherous," Claire said. "Why don't you keep the limo after I'm dropped? It has chains. I'll have your car driven up when the roads clear."

"Thanks. I might. Let's see how bad this gets."

A waitress appeared with coffee. Dave continued the conversation they started in the limo. "Do you want me to handle Geneva on my own? Or do you want to join me?"

"No way. I don't know how to deal with those bureaucrats. Partnering's your strong suit." Claire poured a small amount of milk into her coffee. She scrutinized the cup for a few seconds before looking back to Dave. "Is your single status going to affect your focus?"

"I'm not single."

"But you're not living at home."

"It's… a hiccup. The love of my life is at home in Fort Collins. We'll fix things."

"Distracting, though."

"Emotionally, yes. But God spared me to dive deeper into the work. We're doing a very good thing and it needs my full attention."

"That's what happened? God spared you?"

"How else do you explain the odds of getting pulled out of the security line for a hand check for the first time in ten years? If that doesn't happen, I'm on that plane with Evan."

"That's true. God or not, someone was definitely looking out for you."

"I believe it was God."

"Who knows?" she said. "Some things are best kept a mystery."

"Maybe so."

"Anyway, I'm happy you have a guardian angel whether from God or not," she continued. "We're at a critical juncture. The partnership absolutely needs you. And we need you one hundred percent focused."

"Trust me. Coordinating the bureaucracy with the World Health Organization has my full attention. There's a lot to it without Evan's help. I'm a little concerned about taking my eye off the ball at the office, but I'll figure it out."

"Jennifer's good back-up. That's why I let you have her."

"The engineering team fights her."

"Little boys with toys don't like women driving the train."

"Unfortunately, there's some truth to that."

"You've always seemed immune to that kind of sexism, Dave. Makes you more endearing than you should be." She smiled as she opened her menu.

Dave looked at the menu but did not see it. He thought of Sheila's words. Something was in the works that could cure Liv. But Sheila's backdoor cloud communication channel to him was gone. Claire very likely knew what Sheila wanted to tell him. And probably knew about their communications. She would not tell him she knew because that would be admitting to spying on them. Now, it could be weeks before Sheila got back to him. He needed to find a way to get Claire to help, to tell him what Sheila wanted to tell him.

"So what else is on your plate?" he asked.

"Aside from the getting the firmware integrated with your product, we have a few other surprises in the works."

"Like a cure for AIDS?"

She peered over her menu. "Somebody tell you that?"

"Just makes sense. The rate in West Africa is skyrocketing since Ebola overwhelmed their healthcare systems."

"A cure for AIDS is incredibly ambitious. No one has even come close to a real solution."

"The kind of mountain you like to climb, isn't it, Claire? Who would have thought a malaria vaccine was do-able a few years ago? AIDS is a natural next step on the roadmap."

She put the menu down. "Officially, we don't have such a program. If we did, it would be strictly company confidential."

"We have a non-disclosure agreement."

"Specific to the PDNA project. Doesn't cover anything else."

"So let's expand the non-disclosure to cover it."

"There's nothing to disclose."

The waitress returned. Claire ordered the Moroccan salad and Dave selected a bowl of white chicken chili.

"There's a reason I asked," he said after the waitress left. "I thought you might make an exception to help me out."

"With AIDS?"

"You said you don't want me distracted. Well, I'm distracted."

"It's not business?"

"We could make it business."

"What is it?"

He hesitated briefly. "It's personal. But I need your promise that it stays between us."

"Sure." She leaned slightly forward, her eyebrows knitted.

"I need to find a cure or at least something that does a better job of holding it back," he said.

"AIDS?"

"Yes. It's still HIV, but it's the same issue."

Her eyes widened. "Is that why Mel threw you out? You have it?"

"No. Not me."

"Mel?"

"It's tougher than even that."

Claire sat back, her jaw dropping slightly. "Dear God, Dave."

"She's on her second drug regimen. She developed resistance to the first one and it looks like it might be happening again."

"That's concerning. You may want to look into experimental treatments. Expensive, but you should have plenty after the Prodeus public offering."

"I know that. And I'll do my part to make it happen. But I need your help in finding new drugs. Now. Not later."

She pondered him. "Maybe downstream. There's nothing right now."

"So you're working on something?"

She looked at him. She sipped her coffee. She looked out the window. "The snow's not letting up. You'll need the limo."

"Just tell me there's some kind of hope."

She turned back to face him. "I'll bet you've read everything written about the science in this, Dave. What do you think?"

Dave's grip tightened on his coffee mug. "Treatable," he answered. "Not curable."

McQuaid nodded. "That's the way I see it, too."

"But treatment's almost impossible with drug resistance," Dave said, choking down anger, mostly at himself for letting Claire in on Liv's secret in exchange for nothing.

"Almost," she said grimly.

"So can you help?"

"No."

Dave stared at Claire. She stared back. Finally, he looked outside, gazing at the snowflakes melting slowly on the window.

CHAPTER 7

Peggy's Cove, Nova Scotia
October 28 - 4:05 p.m. Atlantic Time

Seagull cries echoed along the shore. East across the cove that opened into Margaret's Bay and then the Atlantic Ocean, signs of impending nightfall appeared as the lowest layer of the horizon began to darken.

Marie raced along the rocky beach, her tiny, pink bare feet finding the soft sand in between the rocks. When she paused to catch her breath, her feet sunk into wet, black sand at the tide's ebb. It smelled and looked dirty here, like a gas station. Her mother told her it was from the plane. She could still see the search boats bobbing in and out of view in the distant waters of the inlet. The skinny ten-year-old remained fascinated by the sheer number of boats deployed. Mom's small coffee shop in the parlor on the first floor of their old Victorian home had buzzed every morning for over a week. Most of the people had been very nice and Marie had been careful with her manners.

Fr. LaBonte had been over often. Marie liked that. Fr. LaBonte was very kind to her and her mother. They needed him around this week, especially when the crying started. Marie did not like the crying. It made her cry, too. They talked about identifying the bodies. Marie did not want to know about the bodies. She watched a boat unload some in town a few days earlier. Someone unzipped one of the black body bags to show some official. It was all white, blue, and swollen, not really like a person at all. A black hole peered out of one of its eye sockets. Marie vomited on the planks outside the drug store.

Shaking her head to make the memories go away, the ten-year-old ran twenty yards down the beach to an untouched spot where the sand glistened white in the late afternoon sun. Springing from both feet, she splashed into the icy water, squealing with delight. Suddenly concerned, she stopped long enough to glance back at the house and make sure her unauthorized escape remained undiscovered. Her father would "blister her backside" if he caught her. Not seeing her parents or big brother, she began leaping over the small waves as they licked the shore.

"Ouch!" the ten year old shouted as her foot came down on something hard in what should have been soft sand.

Eighteen inches below the foaming surf, the edge of a gray rock peeked out of the sand. Marie bent down for a closer look. She hesitated to touch it as its image quivered mirage-like from the gentle wave action. The ache pulsing in her bruised foot intensified and she angrily reached down and yanked the rock from its repose.

She turned to throw it at the cluster of boulders she had navigated just a few moments earlier. The slick surface pressing against her fingertips caused her to pause in mid-wind-up.

She held a small black plastic box, not a rock at all. Padding over to a large flat boulder, she sat down to examine her find. Brushing away sand and small pieces of shell, she ran her hands over it. She turned the box upside down and sideways, finding several small buttons molded into the hard plastic. She pressed the one on top and nothing happened. She shook the box and held it against her ear. She heard nothing. She pressed the big button in front. A picture of a battery with a narrow bright red section appeared on the front of the box. Below the image, it said "5% charged." Marie realized she had found a phone.

She ran her fingers around the screen. The battery image went away, replaced by a box that said: "Low battery warning. 5% of battery remaining." She tapped the button below the message that said "Dismiss." Words appeared on the screen, but Marie had a hard time making them out in the reflection from the sun setting over her shoulder. She scooched around the rock, putting the sunset in front of her.

As if by magic, the black outline of the words blossomed and intensified before her, their edges becoming crisp and the print bold.

"Smoke's let up. They must have been able to open the cockpit windows. We're flying awfully close to the ocean. Have to wonder if this is sabotage. If it is, my team may be the target. Pilot just announced we're landing in Halifax. I can see the runway lights. Seems I've written this for myself. Better safe than sorry…"

Marie paused her reading as she hissed a frightened breath through clenched teeth. The image of the bloated body flashed back through her mind.

A new message popped up on the screen, blocking the other content.

Low Battery
Less Than 5% of Battery Remaining

Again she tapped the "dismiss" button below the warning and it went away.

"… Bad news. We flew past the airfield. Pilots couldn't keep us straight. Looked like the right wing would smash into the runway. We pulled up at the last second. Smoke pouring from under the cockpit door. As bad as before. Starting to come from the cabin vents now, too. The pilots cannot possibly see up there. As long as the electrical systems hold up, we have a shot. If I don't make it - if you find this -- please take this to some authority outside the United States' sphere of influence…"

Marie had no idea what a sphere of influence was.

"US authorities cannot be entrusted with this. The contents of the files on this phone may be the only hope to stop a horrible atrocity. If they have killed us, then our files will have been destroyed or archived where no one..."

Low Battery
Less Than 5% of Battery Remaining

She tapped the Dismiss button again.

"...no one will find them. If this phone survives us, please... The lights have just gone out. The electrical system. We need you now, God. It's this or prayers. This is my prayer. It can save others. Many, many others. There's fire now. The floor in back just erupted. Hot. People screaming..."

Very Low Battery - Please Connect to Power

She remembered the people crying at the coffee shop. As tears filled her eyes, she again tapped the Dismiss button.

"... Please take seriously. Take to someone who can be trusted..."

Fr. LaBonte, thought Marie.

"Look inside, you'll underst... "

The image of a battery with a red end on it appeared again on the screen. A new warning message appeared below it:

Please Connect to Power

Then the screen went black. Marie tapped around it. Nothing. The battery was dead.

Pondering the blank screen, Marie relived the images of the past several days, the body bags, the vacant bloodshot eyes of bereaved families, the empty eye socket.

She ran back to the house, hugging the box to her chest. She would take it to Father LaBonte. As the rear screen door squeaked behind her and slammed, her father called to her.

"Marie! Marie, is that you?"

She froze at the kitchen sink.

"Marie!" her father repeated.

She could hear his heavy footsteps clomping toward the kitchen. "Yes, papa, it's me," she called back.

"Where have you been?" His voice grew louder as he walked down the old hardwood in the hallway.

Marie scrambled to shove the phone into the back of the kitchen drawer where they kept the plastic bags. She had just finished shutting the drawer when her father entered the room.

"I was playing outside."

Her father looked down at the sand on her still bare feet. "Were you at the beach? What have I told you about the beach?"

He approached her, his arm cocked back across his chest, ready to backhand her. He smelled like beer. He always smelled like beer.

"No, sir, I wasn't," she said quickly, her hands now raised in front of her, poised to protect her face and head.

He looked again at her feet. The sand looked dry. There was plenty of sand in the yard. "You know better, right?"

"Yes, sir."

Her father studied her for a moment longer. He dropped his threatening arm to his side. "It's getting late. You need to stay in for the night. It'll be bedtime soon. I don't want mama finding you up when she finishes at the shop."

He turned and walked toward the living room where the TV played a re-run of "NCIS."

Relieved, Marie thought about retrieving the phone from the drawer, but she did not want to risk getting caught. She ran upstairs to her room. There, she thought about all the people on the plane, about how she would not be able to help now. Her father could never know she disobeyed.

She curled up on the bed, still in her clothes. Folding her hands in front of her lips, she felt her own warm, wet breath on them as she mumbled prayers for the victims and their families.

"…and dear God, please don't let that man's family see his eye. And please, please forgive me for not turning in the phone."

A few minutes later, she had cried herself to sleep.

CHAPTER 8

Lokoma village
October 29, 2:35 pm GMT

Hamara Karanja squatted beside Sara. She lay sweating profusely on a sleep mat spread on the hard dirt floor. Light crept through the thatch overhead, streaking Sara's five-year-old frame with splotches of brightness. His sinewed hand stroked her hair and temples. Her skin felt soft, smooth and frighteningly hot to his touch.

"Papa," she whispered, her wide eyes gazing at his silhouette in the dim hut, "I don't want to be sick anymore."

He reached for a clear, plastic bottle of warm water beside him. "Drink this, Sara," he encouraged as he placed the spout to her lips.

"Nooo," she moaned.

"Dear, you need to. We have to keep water in you or you could get sicker."

"Papa, I don't think I can get sicker."

"It will help make you better."

Conceding, she pursed her lips to receive the water and Hamara tilted the bottle slightly to allow the water to dribble over her lips and tongue. He had sent Jacob for ice at the community room earlier and he wondered why he was not back yet.

"How's that?" he asked his daughter.

"I think I have to go to the bathroom again."

"Are you sure?"

In the dimness, he could see her shake her head affirmatively. He put an arm under her shoulder and helped her up. The amulet strung around her neck caught on the mat. He disdainfully yanked it free; Mariama had insisted on it. She argued that, at worst, it would do no harm. Many of the Lokoma thought the cowry shell amulet could draw the fever out of a body.

Sara tried to wobble to her feet, but Hamara put another arm under her knees and lifted her into the air. He carried her out the door of the hut, leaning forward over her, trying to cast the shadow of his head and shoulders on her. In this way, he hoped to protect her eyes from the bright sunlight.

He walked ten yards to the common latrine. The stench always peaked at this time of day, the heat bringing the odors to life. He carried her inside and set her down on the small wooden commode. As soon as she settled, she let out a small howl. He heard the gushing of her bowels pouring into the stagnant water below. He steeled himself against the smell and kept a gentle hand on her shoulder as she shivered from weakness and fever.

Her little body had grown gaunt, her cheekbones and jaw over-pronounced as the fat stores and water that once puffed her face had now diminished to dangerously low levels. Through eye sockets deepened by this depletion, enormous brown eyes, glistening with tears, looked up at Hamara. She inhaled a deep swallow of the stale air and squeezed out a grateful smile as her head bobbed weakly on her small, frail neck. Her face creased again into pain. She tucked her chin into her chest and bent forward as more drained into the pit.

The quinine tablets Guerra brought had already run out. No more were available. Perhaps it was not malaria because Sara had never really responded adequately to the short treatment regimen. Damn this jungle, Hamara cursed to himself as he thought of all the disease that filled it.

He had asked how western medicine might treat her differently. In an elders meeting, one of the elders said he understood that western hospitals hooked people to intravenous lines and filled their veins with medicine to manage the disease. Hamara had asked how they could do the same. He received only blank looks, then a comment that it was impossible.

"We have no way to do this, Pa," Musa said, using the term of respect reserved for chiefs and diviners. "The fluids would have to be both sterile and refrigerated. And we would need the intravenous equipment. None of that is even available."

"What about Freetown?" the chief had asked.

"Certainly they would have this equipment at the hospital there," offered another elder.

"Where is the priest now?" challenged Musa.

Hamara looked upon his lifelong friend as though he saw a stranger. "Dead, Musa. Kidnapped and executed. You know that."

"She been shot by a witch, Pa," Musa persisted. "Maboru is needed. A traditional healing. The priest is in the afterlife with our ancestors, and they must be fightin' over your betrayal."

Hamara leaned in close to Musa and spoke softly. "That nonsense defies science."

"Science defies generations of learning by our ancestors. The ancestors remain around us watching, protecting us from the devils that fill the forest. Trying to bring us back to who we once were"

"And who were we?"

"A proud, ancient tribe with spirits that kept us well -- as long as we remained faithful to our ancestors."

"They did not save Ketta."

The elders grew silent. Musa studied his calloused hands for a moment, and then spoke. "All of us understand the anguish of losing a child. Every one of us has been touched by this scourge as either parent or sibling. It's not something we can understand. Perhaps, Pa, the spirit world needed her. Perhaps she even left to watch over us."

Hamara had no answer, thinking only that he wanted to feel her in his arms again, wanted to squeeze her close and find a way to keep her safe.

So now he stood in the pit latrine watching another daughter quivering with fever and deteriorating. They had to go to Freetown. He could not allow her to continue to suffer. He could not risk losing her. The rebel threat caused him to hesitate, but the others could manage without him for a few days.

After Hamara re-situated Sara on the sleep mat, Jacob arrived with ice. "The icemaker was almost empty again. I had to wait for more to be made."

Exhausted, Sara nodded off to sleep after a few minutes. Hamara met with his wife Mariama and Jacob outside.

"We need to get her to Freetown," he said.

"Finally," said Mariama with relief.

"Jacob, we could use your help," Hamara said.

Jacob pulled nervously at the pleats of his dark green shorts. "What about the rebels? What if we need to fight?"

"The bandits have moved southwest of here," Hamara said firmly. He did not think of the roving bands as rebels since the ceasefire; he viewed them as pure criminals out for plunder. "They have no reason to come back this way. Even if that happens, we'll be back long before they could re-deploy to this area."

"What if you're wrong?"

Hamara had entertained the same question, but he knew he needed to show confidence, as both father and village chief. "I'm not wrong. And if I were, the last thing any of us should do is try to fight the automatic weapons of these bandits with our machetes and arrows. The elders know to run. We can rebuild again. These huts are not worth the lives of our children. We'll get the land back; they can't destroy that."

Jacob thought for a moment. "What about my mother?"

"I spoke with her. She wants to stay here with your grandparents."

"But I thought she wanted to leave."

"No, Jacob, she's not ready for that."

"I'm staying with her."

"I need you, son."

Jacob's dark eyes narrowed, blood rushing to his face. "So does my mother. Your first wife."

He turned and walked off rapidly, fists clenched, shoulders hunched forward and his little boy legs churning.

CHAPTER 9

Leonardo Da Vinci Airport, Rome
October 29, 5:15 pm Central European Time

The high-pitched whistle of jet engines and the smell of jet fuel bombarded the carabiniere as he approached the tail of the plane. The humidity of Rome's late summer shimmered on the black tarmac, making it look as though it were floating.

It's better than directing traffic at the Colosseum, the carabiniere thought.

He wore the standard dark blue uniform of Italy's state police, accessorized with a white shoulder belt and a red stripe down the side of each trouser leg. A Beretta PM12-S2 submachine gun dangled over his right shoulder on a narrow black leather strap. As he bent to walk under the plane's cargo ramp, his right arm pressed the Beretta against the side of his chest to keep it from bouncing off his leg.

On the other side of the cargo ramp, he straightened up. A harried luggage ramp supervisor greeted him. The cargo belt on the ramp was not moving. A cheap pine coffin sat on the end of it. Gesturing, the ramp supervisor led the carabiniere up a short flight of metal stairs to the platform at the end of the ramp. He kicked the coffin and stepped back.

The cop stared at him, apparently unconvinced by the story being told. The supervisor then bent down and knocked on the coffin. A few seconds later, a barely discernible thump seemed to come from the box.

"Open it," the cop said.

The ramp supervisor waved one of his crew up. The man had a large crowbar and crudely stabbed the edge of the coffin's lid.

"Be careful," said the carabiniere. "Something's alive in there."

Within thirty seconds, the worker finished prying the lid off. Inside, a man, gagged and bound, pleaded with his eyes through narrow slits.

Bending down, the carabiniere unpinned a note from the man's shirt. "For the Pope only," he read out loud, a puzzled look on his face. He checked the man's shirt pocket and found a small plastic packet labeled 'quinine sulphate'.

Fr. Jim watched the man lean toward him. Please remove the gag, he thought. Instead, the man searched his pockets. Gasping weakly, Jim felt his lungs close up again; his head grew very light and he blacked out one more time, his memory drifting back decades to his native Belfast – when they still called him Sean.

Sean jerked free of Mike, dashing into the street. He held no thought of danger to himself, only the well-being of the girls and their mother. But Mike anticipated his move. The older boy clipped Sean behind the ear with a heavy black cudgel.

As he stumbled onto the wet cobblestones, his head spinning from the blow, Sean saw the woman and her children leave the building. The husband, dressed impeccably in a suit with white shirt and orange tie, held one arm around his wife's waist. In his other arm, he carried his two year old whose frail pink arms tightly enfolded her father's neck.

Beside them walked a teenage girl, her angelic image filling the young man's head, her slightly freckled alabaster complexion ethereal under a wreath of auburn hair. She cuddled close to her dad, cooing up at her sister — and then she smiled across the street at him. Their eyes met and he froze under her gentle gaze. Her emerald eyes seemed to cut straight through to his soul.

In his twilight state, Sean crawled forward, stones of the street cutting again into the palms of his hands. As he attempted to rise to his feet, his head jerked back, Mike's hand wrapped tightly around his mouth.

"Ya done good, little brother," Mike whispered in his ear. "Now just watch your work in action."

And then the family picture before him instantly transformed to fire. The heat from the explosion enveloped him, as tongues of fire singed his eyebrows. The father and the other bodyguard lay shaken where they had been thrown more than ten yards from the car.

Sean wanted to run toward the car, but Mike pulled him the other way. They ran and young Sean cried quietly, the wailing of the anguished father filling his ears.

Fr. Jim's eyes blinked open again. He inhaled through his nose and mouth for the first time in a day, his gag finally removed. Above him, the carabiniere finished speaking on his cell phone.

"D'acordo," he told the ramp supervisor. "Let's get him out of here. The Vatican wants him in their infirmary."

"Who is he?" asked the supervisor.

"I don't know. He flew from Freetown in cargo at over thirty-five thousand feet. And he did it gagged. He's lucky he survived."

"And he's addressed to the Pope," commented the supervisor.

"Hell, maybe the note has assembly instructions," said the carabiniere. "Maybe he's the second coming in a do-it-yourself kit."

Too weak to speak, Jim slipped back into unconsciousness.

CHAPTER 10

Lokoma Village
October 30, 5:35 a.m. GMT

Jacob slept lightly beside his mother in their hut. In the pre-dawn darkness, distant thunder awakened him. He stepped through the beaded doorway into the muggy darkness, quickly recognizing the ominous rumble of distant mortar fire. His father said the fighting had moved southwest, but this sounded like it had shifted again toward the village. If it had, someone needed to warn everyone. Jacob was the son of the chief. He needed to find out.

In the darkness, he heard movement from the jungle behind the hut. Probably just monkeys, he thought. The movement had not come from the direction of the trail. A vantage point atop a barren hill lay at the end of the trail, a ten minute jog away. From there, he would be able to locate the fighting by watching the flashes in the jungle below.

He listened for the movement again. Nothing but the whispered flapping of ferns and leaves blowing in the easy breeze. Carefully, he stepped behind the concession of huts and moved toward the jungle. He looked at his father's hut. No one there. They had left in the truck in the late afternoon to take Sara to hospital in Freetown.

"Jesus," Jacob whispered in the dark, "please make Sara well. She doesn't deserve to suffer. She's sweet and she loves you. If she is paying for the sins of our parents, punish me instead. I'm stronger."

He could barely discern the ferns that marked the edge of the village clearing and the beginning of the trees. He watched their gentle, wind-blown movement closely, careful that they were indeed ferns. He squeezed his eyes shut for an instant.

"I'm scared, Lord. Help me find the courage of a chief's son. Help me to protect the village."

Opening his eyes, he found they were better adapted to the dark now. He discerned the beginning of the trail about ten yards distant. After trotting over, he hesitated for a moment, filling his chest with air before beginning his run into the deeper darkness of the forest.

Less than ten minutes later, Jacob arrived huffing and puffing at the vantage point, just under a mile from the village. He climbed over rocks to the top of what was an earthen outcropping. He could hear the rhythmic bleating of jungle insects, but the thunder was gone. Maybe it had not been mortar fire after all. He sat down on a boulder and pondered the darkness. No flashes. No man-made noises. No thunder.

In the dark jungle below him, he saw the lights of fireflies and occasionally pairs of eyes appeared nearby. They were animal, not human.

Regardless, Jacob kept very still. They could belong to a harmless monkey or a dangerous wild boar. Whatever they were, he did not want to be of interest to them.

At first, Jacob just sat on the boulder. Then, he put his hands behind him and leaned back. Finally, he curled up on one side, telling himself to listen. Within moments, he slept.

CHAPTER 11

Lokoma Village
October 30, 6:12 a.m. GMT

Ani stirred on her mat. Her eyes still closed, she reached for Jacob, but she found only an empty spot beside her. She sat up and saw the first gray light of dawn slipping through the strings of beads and cowry shells that acted as the door to her hut. She heard footsteps outside. Jacob, she thought.

Standing, she wrapped a small blanket around her shoulders to protect against the damp morning chill. Pushing the beads aside, she peered through a thick mist and saw Jacob by her parents hut with another boy. Both carried machetes. She started to call to him when she caught his face in full profile. It was not Jacob.

She tiptoed back into her hut to grab the spear Hamara had taught her to use. Coming back outside, she pushed the beads aside and ran quietly on bare feet toward the two boys that now entered her parents' home, their machetes raised. She tilted the spear up, prepared to attack.

Then she felt rapid-fire blows to her body and head that knocked her to the ground. Someone yanked the spear from her grip. She struggled to stand, but more blows knocked her back down. She grabbed the ground and pulled herself back toward her hut, only to be kicked again and again on her back and legs. She finally crawled under the beads at her hut's entrance and saw the knife she wanted, but her attackers had her by the ankles. She reached for the knife but it slid out of range as they pulled her back. She screamed in anger and frustration, rolling over and kicking wildly at the assailants. Until a rifle butt slammed into her skull.

As dawn broke, the chirping of the birds crescendoed easing Jacob into wakefulness. He peered through the leaves of trees over his head and saw first light glistening in the dew. Suddenly realizing that his mother would soon discover he was gone, he raced back down the trail to the village.

He hoped that if he moved quickly enough, he would arrive before anyone else wakened, but as he got closer, he thought he heard loud voices from the village. As he came within the last hundred yards, he recognized the sounds as keening and wailing. Someone had died. Oh no, he thought, maybe they discovered him missing and thought he had died.

As he emerged from the jungle, he quickly understood that something very wrong had happened. The village teemed with stunned people praying, cursing and crying. At his grandparents' hut, he saw blood trickling over the doorstop. Going in, he discovered the bodies of his grandparents, chopped to death as they slept. His grandmother's arm lay separated from her body on her husband's shoulder as though she had reached out to him in their last moment. Both of them had their eyes wide open with the final flutter that death brings.

Young Jacob collapsed to the floor, stunned and horrified. He started to reach out to re-attach his grandmother's arm, but tears blinded him and he hesitated. Suddenly, he jumped to his feet. "Mother!" he screamed, racing out the door to the next hut.

She was not there. In a few moments, someone saw Jacob's panic and told him she had been carried off the by the attackers.

"What will happen to her now?" he asked.

"Someone will probably make her his slave, maybe even a wife," said the man who told him of the kidnapping.

"I have to save her," he said.

"We should all wait for Pa Karanja to return. He'll know what to do."

"Then where was he?" Jacob said angrily.

"Jacob, the Lord must have been watching out for him. Had he been here, they surely would have killed him, Mariama and your sisters. That is a certainty. The chief and his family are always the first victims in attacks like this. It's a miracle they missed you."

"I had gone off in the jungle."

The man looked at Jacob curiously before continuing. "They may think they did kill the family. The killers were just children."

The man continued to ponder Jacob.

"I thought I heard noises," Jacob said, anticipating the man's questions.

"What kind of noises?"

"Mortar fire."

"Did you find it?"

"No, there was nothing. I fell asleep on an outcropping a little more than a kilometer from here."

"God must have been watching out for you."

Jacob looked around the village: bodies being dragged and lined up outside, blood seeping from huts and soaking into the ground. The wailing ebbed and flowed with each new discovery or realization.

"Why did He not watch out for them?" he asked behind wet eyes.

CHAPTER 12

Aldrich Mountain Lab, Cameron Pass
October 30, 4:15 a.m.

Sleep did not come easily for Sheila. She feared that the program to cure HIV and AIDS risked going completely off the rails. For years, she had been an enthusiastic supporter – and driver – of the plan. She, Jennifer, Eldridge and Claire all could share credit on the architecture of the plan to deliver Sheila's designer protein, Vif-D, as a Trojan horse inside the new malaria vaccine. Arguably, it crossed the line on hard and fast rules of pharmaceutical ethics. But the plan would eradicate AIDS with no cost in human lives.

Until now.

Sheila designed Vif-D to effectively morph in the body from HIV's natural Vif cells through her team's bio-engineering. The replacement of the Vif protein with Vif-D did two very important things: first, it dramatically shortened the period between introduction of HIV and sero-conversion to AIDS, leading to death within months - except in the presence of the CEM15-D gene designed by the Aldrich. That exception was the key to the whole cure.

CEM15-D completely destroyed the effectiveness of HIV once Vif-D allowed access to the T cells that managed immunity. The CEM15-D gene morphed from the natural CEM15 gene already present in the human body. Natural CEM15 provided only a weak ineffective defense against HIV as part of human T cells.

In the plan agreed upon, Vif-D needed to be delivered as part of a two-step solution that would eradicate HIV cells in the human body. The second step, injection of the CEM15-D designer gene, was essential to that eradication. In Sheila's simian experiments, CEM15-D completely overcame Vif-D, bringing a complete halt to the proliferation of SIV cells, the simian version of HIV, effectively starving the disease out.

The trick was that the CEM-15 gene that existed naturally in the body, not Sheila's designer version, could not out-duel Vif-D, and the immune system's T-cells quickly succumbed to it. That was why it was so essential the designer CEM15-D be injected as soon as possible after the initial injection of Vif-D.

She opened the page in her notebook that she labeled "Recipes for life and death". She read each one again as though reviewing them would get Claire to change her mind.

> **Current state of things: Vif + CEM15 = AIDS victim dying over a period as long as ten years**

Interim state of things: Vif-D + CEM15 = AIDS victim dead within four to six months

Goal state: Vif-D + CEM15-D = AIDS eradicated once and for all.

But Sheila's team could not complete CEM15-D until antibodies were available from those injected with Vif-D. Those antibodies were essential to completion of a CEM15-D designer gene. With technology licensed from the University of Texas, Sheila could characterize an antibody's DNA sequence in a few weeks instead of the year normally required. With that information, they could customize CEM-15D for the specific population's phenotype in just a few more weeks.

For those in the pilot program receiving the malaria vaccine injection with the Trojan horse Vif-D in it, they had less than 120 days to get the CEM15-D injection before the virulent AIDS caused by Vif-D killed them.

This, Sheila agreed, would not have been a problem if CEM15-D successfully adhered to the body's T-cells. It did not.

In the lab and in chimps they had, but in human subjects, adherence problems had developed. For some reason, CEM15-D genes did not attach to the T-cells in the human body, even though they attached in test tubes. Sheila and her team had worked on the problem non-stop for weeks, but knew it could be months before resolution. She felt supremely confident it would be fixed, but a lot of trial and error still lay ahead of her team in finding the right chemical formulation.

So Sheila had gone separately to Claire and to Eldridge to insist on a delay in the implementation of the Trojan horse in the vaccine. Both insisted on maintaining the current timeline, expressing their confidence in Sheila's ability to solve the problem in time.

But she and her team had not yet solved it. And once the malaria vaccine with the Trojan horse was delivered, Sheila had only weeks to fix the adherence issue and build the CEM15-D gene with antibodies from the field. Sheila argued with Claire that the risk was too high, much higher than any of them had ever anticipated. The Trojan horse needed to be delayed.

She remembered Claire's face on the video chat the night before. She never recalled seeing her long-time mentor that cold and determined. Claire's emerald eyes, normally functioning to engage people, seemed to say "back off" in the firmest way.

"You do your job, Sheila, and stop rocking the boat." Claire said. "We're in the business of life and death. And I'm the only that gets to play God."

The conversation left Sheila with a very empty feeling and a deep sense of horror. She had only weeks to solve the CEM15-D adherence problem. If she did not, tens of thousands – and possibly more - would begin dropping dead of AIDS within four months.

CHAPTER 13

Lokoma Village
October 30, 11:47 a.m. GMT

Hamara Karanja stopped the truck at the edge of the village. Black bodies mutilated and encrusted with dried blood lined the wooden porch of the community building

"No!" he shouted, slamming the steering wheel over and over again with his fists, "God, no!" He jumped from the vehicle, running into Lokoma.

In the passenger seat, Mariama pulled three year old Emma closer to her, rocking her back and forth. She thanked God they had left Sara behind at the clinic in Freetown. At first, she shed quiet tears, but quickly broke into huge sobs as she scanned the carnage before her.

"Jacob! Ani!" Hamara called repeatedly as he ran among the thatch work.

As he approached their hut, a beefy hand landed on his back. Another grabbed his shoulder and turned him. It was Musa, the bloated elder. The man stood before him like a risen Buddha, his girth peeking from beneath the shirttail of a khaki bargain from the Red Cross store.

"They're alive," he said, the whites of his eyes lined with bright red from crying.

"Where?" Hamara blurted.

"Not here, Pa," Musa said gently, one hand still on his chief's shoulder.

"Where, Musa?" he asked, fearing the answer.

"They took Ani."

"Who took her?"

"Rebel militia."

"Boys then?"

"Yes."

"Where's Jacob?" Hamara continued, trying to contain the explosion of anguish inside.

"He was here when it ended. We think he ran into the jungle."

"Did anyone see in which direction?"

"No. There's more."

Hamara said nothing, but dropped his hands to his side. He shifted his shoulders and inhaled deeply.

"Ani's parents are dead."

Hamara's breath caught. Even though he and Ani were no longer married, they had been like his own parents, both long gone from malaria.

"How?"

Musa shook his head and averted his eyes.

"How, Musa?"

Musa closed his eyes as he spoke, "Machetes."

Hamara placed his hands over his face. He wanted to scream, to curse at God. Instead, he remembered his people would be looking to him. He dropped his hands and raised his chin.

"Do we know why they came?" he asked calmly.

"We think they wanted you, Pa. We hope they believe they got you. They were just boys, few older than Jacob. They would not have attacked unless they thought you were here. "

Hamara's eyes rounded into a look half-insane. He paced in front of Musa.

"Your concern for Sara saved you," Musa said.

"I should have stopped this."

"There was no way to know."

"I told Jacob they would not come."

Hamara stopped pacing. His voice softened. He looked out into the village. "Who else is hurt?"

"Perhaps fifteen, including Siro..." Siro, the most senior of the elders: Hamara's most steadfast friend and supporter. "... and his wife."

"Who else?" Hamara asked, his voice breaking.

"His son and his family."

"The baby."

"Everyone."

Hamara turned his back completely to Musa now. He struggled to hold back tears, tears that would show weakness. Musa walked up and tenuously placed an arm around Hamara's shoulder. Musa blinked back the tears that threatened to return to his own eyes.

Hamara reached a hand up and grasped Musa's wrist, pulling it more tightly to his shoulder. Hamara thought of Jesus. He struggled to understand how an all-loving God could have let this massacre happen. First Fr. Jim, he thought. Now this.

Hamara let go of Musa's wrist. He slipped to his knees in the blood-streaked dirt. An invisible fist plunged into his chest wrenching his heart into a twisted knot of physical and emotional anguish. The fist plunged deeper, pushing up through his throat, the anguish first surfacing as a soft whimper.

He bent forward, placing his forehead on the dirt. Suddenly, he lifted his head and looked skyward.

"Whyyyyyyy?" he screamed.

CHAPTER 14

Liv's Journal
November 2, 10:20 pm Mountain Time

Mom's crying again tonight. I can hear her. She thinks I'm asleep. I was 'til I heard her crying. She's very quiet about it, but I have a sixth sense for her. We're connected in a spiritual way.

Used to be that way with Dad. When I was little. That's what Mom says. I don't remember. Second grade is a million years ago. He turned complete workaholic around then. Grandmom says he always overdid everything. Worked non-stop for good grades and a letter in football. A nerdy football player. He's still a nerd.

He learned to play the guitar really well, too. She said he never kept friends around 'cause he stayed too serious, working even when he didn't need to. They liked him enough – he probably bored them to death. Kids want to have fun.

Mom taught him about fun. He told me that. He said I made him feel young again, too. We had lots of fun when I was little. Riding bumper boats in Estes Park, hitting baseballs in the batting cage, riding bikes. He wouldn't read to me much, but when he did, he did these voices for every character. I'd laugh so hard. And so would he. Think he stopped doing that 'cause of Mom. She acted hurt 'cause I preferred to have him read. She read to me every night. He read to me once every couple months and got the glory. If I push too hard for Dad to come home, she could get her feelings hurt again. There's enough hurt going around as it is.

What's going on with him anyway? He almost died in that plane with his friend. Any normal person would take it as a strong hint to stay home while he still could. Not Dad. Mom said he feels called to finish his work in Sierra Leone. Called? Guess that makes him Joan of Arc or something. Mom defends him to me. She doesn't believe it, though. Like me, Mom thinks he's running away from us. Why else would she cry every night?

Right now, my chest is pounding. I feel dizzy, too. Maybe it's the meds. They make me feel this way a lot. For the last week or two, I have been so tired again. Skipping a couple days couldn't have hurt that much. I'm back on 'em. I'm lucky I can get 'em. From everything I read, very few of the people in Africa or Asia can get the meds. I'll have to write Jacob about it. If he remembers me. It's been a long time. Now, if he could text...

Of course, what difference do the meds really make if you're going to die anyway? Maybe poor Africans are better off than I am because they know exactly where they stand from the beginning. For me, I feel good one day, bad the next. Feel like I'll live forever one day, like I'm doomed the next. The doctor says my form of HIV might be drug resistant. Which raises the question: how many HIVs are there?

Dad can fix this. He's probably working on it all the time. Or he would be if it wasn't for his stupid job. He knows this stuff. It's biotech. His business.

He's only bothered to see me once since the Charco Broiler. It's like I don't matter. Guess he thinks I'm dying anyway. Why waste his time?

At least, he could try to be here on weekends. Oh, right… Mom doesn't want that. She asked me if I want him home if all he's going to do is sit in front of the computer doing e-mail and reports. Or talk business on the phone. Sure, he makes me mad when he does that, but I'd rather him be around — even if he's just around. I'm kinda mad at Mom about that.

Anyway, guess it's up to me to find out what cures are out there. I'm the only one that really cares about me. They'll be sorry when I die. Mom will be there, crying, blaming Dad. He'll show up at the last minute or call with an apology. Or not. Maybe they'll finally get it; when they see everyone at the funeral crying, maybe they'll realize how they gave up their little girl for stupid jobs and pride.

God, I am so sobbing.

Just heard a toilet flush. Means that Mom's up. She'll check on me. I'd better turn off the light before she catches me crying. That'll only make her worry more. Have to take care of the old immune system, y'know.

CHAPTER 15

Fort Collins High School
November 4, 11:33 a.m.

Outside the classroom window, fat snowflakes floated down through a cold, dreary backdrop of gray, leafless tree silhouettes and snow-laden pine branches. The grayness contrasted with the bright fluorescent track lighting of the classroom. Liv could smell and feel the comforting heat from the radiator that ran the length of the window. Pressing her shoulders up to her neck, she felt the soft cashmere of her white sweater on her skin. She stroked one sleeve with her fingers and felt soothed by the touch. She glanced at the big, round white-faced clock over the blackboard in front: 11:33. Almost lunchtime. The warm fragrance of fresh-baked bread and beef stew wafting under the classroom door from the cafeteria accentuated the empty, hungry feeling in her belly.

She always sat near the back of the class, far from the chalk dust. In the seventh grade, she had discovered that chalk dust aggravated her mild asthma. In the years since, moving toward the back had made school a much more pleasant experience.

Now her asthma seemed not only mild but also totally irrelevant in her life. She struggled to fight off the obsession, praying for peace of mind, running in place in the girls' room, taking deep breaths. None of it worked today. She envisioned her future as bleak as the landscape outside. Her life would be short. She could not have boyfriends. There would be no career or babies in her future. And everyone would hate her and avoid her.

Classes went slowly all morning. None of the lecture content seemed to register. A couple of the teachers had called on her, probably because she was glassy-eyed and inattentive. Somehow, an automatic part of her brain had registered enough to offer answers both times. Looking up, the fuzzy outline of a fluorescent-lit teacher over her, she smelled the chalk dust and the mix of faint teenage body odor and mall-sample cologne as though she had just entered the room. Yet her first answer surprisingly hit the nail on the head. The other was far more vague, but came close enough to generate other discussion in the room while Liv drifted back to think about coping.

After class, she swapped books at her locker and maneuvered down the crowded halls to the library. Alone in the library, the smell of warm bread and gravy again wafted by her. Chelsea had pestered her to join them for lunch, expressing disbelief that Liv would "actually" give up lunch for history research. Liv remained unbending in her commitment and now, sitting at a library workstation, she closed her eyes and inhaled the rich aromas, thinking how hungry she was, wondering if there would be bread and aromas in heaven.

Her fingers remained poised on the keyboard nonetheless, the chatter of the keys signaling progress in her search for information on HIV. If Dad didn't do it, she would do it herself.

HIV Cures. She typed the words into the search box on the monitor. She clicked on the first choice in the results. The words jumped off the page.

> People who catch HIV are increasingly likely to encounter mutant forms of the virus that are able to resist some of the drugs commonly used to treat the infection...
>
> HIV leads to AIDS, which is the symptomatic period for HIV. Untreated, AIDS is a death sentence, but with...

The fear again. The weariness this past week. She just wanted to sleep most of the time.

> ...Untreated, AIDS is a death sentence, but...

Butterflies replaced hunger in her stomach. Her throat constricted painfully and her mouth grew so dry that her tongue stuck to the roof of her mouth.

> ...AIDS is a death sentence, but...

She felt the hard splash of dirt on her face, the thick aroma of the loam filling her head. She tried to cover her face, but her arms could not move. Nothing moved. The dirt felt cold on her skin. Above her, a dark, narrow shaft led to daylight, but shovelfuls of mud kept flying into the hole, filling it, burying her.

> ...AIDS is a death sentence...

She pressed her hands over her face in an open, silent scream. The nightmare had visited at least three times and now it haunted her daytime.

Tears dripped out of her eyes. She blinked them back and clicked the home icon.

...AIDS is a death sentence...

"Please go away," she whispered, "Please."

Finally, the screen refreshed. The offending article disappeared, replaced by the results summary. Clicking randomly, unthinkingly, on sites, her concentration evaporated. Words and pictures flashed in front of her, but she saw them only briefly, quickly clicking to the next search result. No article brought her comfort. No article told her she would be okay. The hourglass icon seemed to spin indefinitely as the pages refreshed slowly through the school's painfully slow servers. So she navigated from article to article at a snail's pace searching desperately for any kind of reassurance. She reached over and laid a hand on top of the monitor, tapping it.

"C'mon. Please help me."

She placed a hand on each side of it, shaking it, causing the picture to wobble. She let go and sat upright. The bottom third of the picture on the monitor curled to the right like an ocean wave. It was not supposed to do that. She feared she had broken it.

Putting her head in her hand, she unconsciously invoked a prayer, "Oh, God, please don't let this happen. This is all I need right now."

She glanced up and the monitor had normalized. A little surprised, she looked toward the ceiling and mouthed a silent "thank you."

The relief she felt at overcoming her momentary tribulation lifted her spirits. For a moment, the fear reduced itself to nagging doubt in the pit of her stomach, but not the overwhelming sensation of hopelessness that had attacked her only moments earlier.

Then, a fresh determination welled up inside her. She pushed the chair away from the workstation and then glared at it.

She spoke quietly to the monitor, "I'll beat this."

She looked around. The library had very few people in it. It was maple colored and quiet. Like a funeral home, she thought. Alone. Fear surged back through her. She grabbed her purse and jumped up.

Liv arrived in the cafeteria for the last 10 minutes of lunch break. She welcomed the company of the loud cacophony of voices and clattering silverware. After buying a warm roll and a diet soda, she sought out Chelsea. Her friend regaled two other girls with whispered tales of furtive adventures, filled with sidebars about male anatomy.

"Do you ever stop thinking about that stuff?" Liv asked as she sat down in the midst of them.

"Liv! You made it! All right. What's up with you, anyway? Research at lunch. That's against some kind of code or something."

Liv pondered Chelsea's half-full plate of beef stew, a once a week cafeteria treat. She plunked the edge of her roll in the gravy.

"Hey! Did I say you could have that?" Chelsea said in mock horror.

"You're so sweet to share," Liv responded as she bit off the hot, gravy-soaked piece of roll.

"We've shared everything else, including chicken pox and mumps forever," Chelsea said. "Doctors ever figure out what happened to you?"

"Dizzy spells from dehydration," she said, hoping the explanation would be accepted. "This is so good," Liv remarked, placing another piece of roll in her mouth.

"It's an STD. That's why you won't talk about it. I always knew you were a slut, Clement."

"Takes one to know one," Liv said, dipping another piece of roll in gravy.

"I guess your appetite's all right."

"I need nutrition after a bout with dehydration."

"Sounds like you need to keep a water bottle with you," Chelsea said. "I've told you that."

Liv nodded.

"So what's so important that you would give up lunch?"

One of the other girls added, "Yeah. What's up with that?"

Liv sipped her soda, buying a few seconds to think. "What's really important is what you're talking about. Don't you ever worry that you'll get some kind of disease? Maybe even AIDS?"

Chelsea burst into laughter and the other girls, except Liv, followed.

"AIDS!" Chelsea said. "Do I act gay to you?"

"You don't have to be gay to get it," Liv said.

"Pretty much," another girl offered. "My mom knows people with AIDS. They're all gay."

"They bring it on themselves," Chelsea said. "They don't wear protection. And they do it in some pretty nasty ways."

"Chelsea!" cried Margret. "Don't go there. I'm still eating."

Liv looked at Chelsea curiously. "I don't know what you mean," she said.

Chelsea leaned forward conspiratorially, "They do it in the wrong…"

She raised her eyebrows while Liv figured it out.

"So gross," Liv said.

All four girls wadded up their faces and looked at each other to make sure everyone felt the same way.

Chelsea again leaned forward. "Could you ever?"

A chorus of "no's" and "never's" ensued. Chelsea and Liv exchanged an awkward glance. Chelsea grew quiet and looked at her plate.

"Look, you guys, gay is okay if that's your thing, but plenty of regular people get AIDS," Liv said. "People get it from blood transfusions or their husbands."

"That's 'cause their husbands are really gay and they're screwing around on them with other gay guys," Margret offered. "And gay is anything but normal."

"Or they don't even have to be gay," Chelsea suggested. "The husbands could be having sex with prostitutes on business trips. Everybody knows prostitutes are lesbos. Otherwise they'd be falling in love with their customers and you should never mess around with people at work. My mother told me that."

Liv studied the group. They would never accept her if they found out. In fact, they would hate her. She blinked back an involuntary tear. Her lips curled and quivered. Composing herself, she tried one more time. "Chelsea, you don't even think about it when you're with boys?"

"The only one I've had sex with is Aidan. He's had lots of girlfriends. None of them had any diseases."

"He told you that?"

"Mm-hmmm. But we're both very faithful now that we have each other."

"But I thought…"

Chelsea interrupted, clearly knowing where this was headed.

"That's not sex," she quickly asserted.

Liv nodded and sipped her drink again. I'm so over, she thought.

"Liv, what's up?" Chelsea said. "You look like you're going to cry."

"I have to go," Liv said, quickly scooping up her books and getting up from the table.

"What's her problem?" Margret asked.

In the girls' restroom down the hall, Liv stood alone in a stall, struggling to stop weeping.

CHAPTER 16

Lokoma Village
November 5, 8:25 a.m. Greenwich Mean Time

Jacob and the other boys walked among the huts. The abandoned village smelled like old fires and faintly of rotting fruit. Jacob wondered if it had always smelled like that. Maybe he had just never noticed. The twinge of homesickness, of longing for Ani and Hamara and his sisters, grew stronger as he breathed in, a weakness forming in the pit of his stomach.

Except for the footsteps of the boys and the occasional movement of animals in the brush, no signs of life existed. Jacob had gone first to Ani's hut, pushing back the strings of beads she had so tediously strung together to hang over the entrance. In the hut's earthen floor, deep and long scrapings marred the ground. He bent down to study them. The ten year old blinked back a tear. His mother must have dug her fingers into the ground in a last attempt to hold on as her kidnappers dragged her out.

"I should have been here," he said, gently running a hand over the same ground his mother had. He dropped to the floor, sitting with his legs crossed, watching the hut that still held his and his mother's clothes and cooking pots.

"Where's mama, God?" he whispered. He dug the fingertips of his right hand into the ground, pulling slowly backward, the horror of his mother's last moments here haunting his imagination.

"Jacob, help me!" The scream reverberated in his head. He threw his hands against his face and pressed with all his might, but the scream would not be pushed out.

"Mama, forgive me." His hands slid down his face, over the fresh pocket cut in his left temple, the spot where the rebel doctor sprinkled medicine on boy soldiers to heal their memories and protect them from forest devils. The fear grew smaller in Jacob when he had the medicine. With Fr. Jim dead, the devils had defeated a great ally of the Lokoma. The priest's God promised good things and loved his enemies. Jacob once thought he could love his enemies, but knew now that he could not.

He crossed his arms on his knees and leaned his forehead on them, looking at the red earth. "Our Father, who art in heaven, hallowed be thy name…" Jacob slowly recited the Lord's Prayer, trying to mean every phrase as Father Jim had taught him. He hoped that if he prayed the prayer of Jesus, God the Father would put everything back the way it was before Christianity came to the village, that Jesus would not turn on him as well.

"…but deliver us from evil…"

"Jacob! Jacob!" His unit commander, a boy of seventeen, threw back the beads. "There you are," he said. "What are you doing? Are you crying? Was this your hut?"

Jacob did not stand. He just looked up, quietly asking God to make him strong now. "No, sir, I'm not crying."

"Is this your hut, Jacob?"

"Yes."

"Who lived here?"

"My mother and I."

The teenage commander, a green sash over his shoulder the only mark of a uniform and command, nodded his head as though he had secret knowledge. "Do you understand what happened here?"

Jacob looked at him puzzled. Wasn't it obvious? "They killed my grandparents and captured my mother."

The teenager, his face and shoulders pocked with untreated acne, squatted and looked kindly at Jacob. "She's gone, too, Jacob. They would not have let her live for long. Only as long as she was useful."

"I don't understand."

"Our enemies use women and throw them away when they're done."

"No. Why would they hurt her?"

"Why not her? They hurt everyone else."

Jacob struggled not to cry, but his face contorted and tears came out anyway. The teenager placed a hand on his shoulder.

"You want to fix this?"

"How?"

"We know who did this. It is a rebel confederation of villages that was jealous of your tribe. The priests brought this curse to you. The Catholic priests and nuns. They brought bad spirits with them. They caused this."

Jacob digested this. If Father Jim had never come, things would have been different. More than one wife would have been okay. Ani and Jacob would have stayed with Hamara and Mariama and the children. But everything else did seem better until the priest died. The priest protected them from the rebels and bandits, from the evil. Jacob wondered if the forest devils had won. Or had his father or even the priest offended Jesus?

"I thought we were the rebels," Jacob said, confused.

"When we found you in the woods, I told you there were many rebel groups. Ours is the good one. We are the soldiers of Allah. We need you to help us fight all the bad ones. The bad ones and the government forces that started this whole thing to destroy our villages. It's the government people, the rich people and their missionary friends, trying to get our land. They and the bad rebels are just in it for themselves."

"I want to help. They have to stop this."

"Don't worry. We can stop them. We know where their villages are. We'll give them some of their own medicine."

Jacob's eyes widened. "Kill them?"

"That's right. You can be part of that. Do to their elders what they had their boys do to your mother and grandparents."

"I don't think so. We have soldiers to do that."

The skinny commander stood and pulled on Jacob's arm. "You are a soldier, Jacob. Remember your blood line. You have the blood of a paramount chief."

Reluctantly, Jacob pushed off the ground and stood.

"What better soldier could we have," the teenager said as he guided Jacob back through the beads.

That night, the boys sat in the village and watched a combination VCR/TV plugged into the old generator. An old gray bearded man, probably almost 40, brought the tape and set it up in the darkness. He stopped by Jacob. For a moment, he pondered the young boy, his eyes penetrating him.

"Your father wasn't there, was he?" he finally said. "He conveniently left before the attack that killed your mother and grandparents."

"She's alive," Jacob said angrily.

Though partially obscured by the evening shadows, the man's features included a big Semitic nose with thick African lips protruding through his beard. A crew-cut of bleached blond hair capped his skull like an obscenity. In spite of the man's ugliness, Jacob could not stop looking at his face and his burning dark eyes.

"That might not be good for her, Jacob. You have to let her go. Avenge her. Be thankful for the opportunities this camp brings you."

He walked away, but Jacob could not stop seeing the eyes burned into his memory like hot coals.

For the fourth time, the boys watched Rambo outfox and terrorize the governing officials who did not understand him, did not appreciate all he had done, the greedy government officials much more interested in their wealth than the good of the people. Rambo destroyed the town of the bad guys. Like the other boys, Jacob could not take his mesmerized eyes off the screen.

CHAPTER 17

Prodeus Headquarters, Loveland, Colorado
November 5, 4:45 p.m. Mountain Time

Dave looked at the new text from Mel as he walked out of his office.

> What happened to the cure from your friend?
> It's been almost two weeks.

He decided to wait to respond until after his meeting with Ed Hepp. It would be the same response he had been texting back for days, the same report that he had no word. Sheila's cloud repository had not been updated since before the funeral. He concluded that either her access had been blocked, as she suspected at Conger's memorial service, or that she thought Aldrich security was reading the content. If the Aldrich had, in fact, discovered the communications, Eldridge Perry or one of the other execs may have even confronted her and told her to stop.

He entered Ed's office. CEO and founder of Prodeus, Ed sat behind his desk, smiling smugly. A heavyset man with thick white hair and Coke bottle bottoms for eyeglasses, he rested his beefy forearms on the desk and folded his thick hands in front of him. The late afternoon sun, peaking wanly through thick cloud cover, glimmered through the window behind him, creating a halo effect around Ed's large head.

"Sit down," Ed said in a sonorous voice.

Dave dropped into one of the blonde wood chairs in front of Ed's desk.

"We never had a chance to talk about Evan's service," Ed asked. "I wanted to go."

"People understand." Dave observed the quaking in Ed's hands. Normally when Ed folded his hands the tremors could not be readily detected. Recently they had become more persistent and more obvious.

"I know he was a mentor to you," Ed said. "Even though I only met him a few times, it was clear he inspired confidence and trust."

"Thanks, I miss him." Dave looked past Ed to the snow covered lawn of Prodeus headquarters that rolled over a hill into fields that collided with the gray rock and scattered pines of the Rockies. High above them, the tip of Longs Peak, glistening with heavy snow, towered more than fourteen thousand feet into an intensely blue sky. Mt Meeker, only slightly lower, rose on the southeast side of Longs Peak and Mt Lady Washington ascended on the northeast. The Aldrich's mountain lab, where Sheila claimed to hold the secret to Liv's well-being, nestled in Cameron Pass to the north and east of the three peaks. .

"So, are you ready to make some money?" Ed asked.

"How do you mean?"

Ed shoved a trembling sheet of paper at him. "You must have said something right at lunch with Claire," Ed said. "This just arrived in purchasing's email."

In his hand, Dave found a purchase order for the first four hundred PDNA units for the Aldrich, not a release to build, but a significant step nonetheless. "Yeess!" Dave exclaimed, pumping his fist.

"Congratulations."

"I'd better call and thank her. Six million dollars is a very nice order."

"I'll say. It's the groundwork we need to leverage an IPO?"

"Isn't it too soon? We're a long way from sustainable profitability."

"Way the markets are, we want to take advantage of them before things get back to normal. Remember how fast things went south in 2000 and again in 2008. We don't want to drag our feet. A big infusion of capital from an IPO will allow us to open up markets a lot faster. That will keep us ahead of any potential competition. An order of this magnitude from a major customer makes us very credible."

Ed sat back in his chair, clumsily folding his shaking hands on his substantial stomach, a grin running from ear to ear.

"What do we do for an underwriter?" Dave asked.

"Dorfmann's been giving that one a lot of cycles," Ed referred to Dan Dorfmann, their chief financial officer. "Thatcher Ripley's the most likely. With Pamela Thatcher's ties to the Aldrich and her understanding of the PDNA opportunities in sub-Saharan Africa, her firm gets what we're doing. We won't have a lot of explaining to do."

"What can I do to help?"

"Just keep running the business. Get the product tested and shipped. Sell it. Cement partnerships that will keep us wealthy well into our old age. Dorfmann and I will take care of the investment community."

As Dave left Hepp's office a few minutes later, he started calculating what an IPO could mean to him, an exercise he seemed to go through any time there was good news. He multiplied potential stock prices by the number of options he held. Even a conservative public offering could easily be worth $2 million pre-tax in his pocket. A good market and strong acceptance by the investment community could mean a whole lot more.

His job now was to keep things on track, to keep from screwing things up. As he turned into his office, he blessed himself and mumbled a short prayer. He ended by saying out loud, "…and don't let me blow this one."

CHAPTER 18

Clement Home
November 6, 4:15 p.m. Mountain Time

Mel Clement studied the spreadsheet on the screen. Another click and another sum appeared at the bottom of the column. She sat back in her study chair and folded her arms. The bank had been good about her leaving early today. Her VP told her she could take whatever time she needed as long as she managed to get her work done.

Her eyes glimpsed the thermometer on the desk. The bottom of the computer screen showed one of the open windows as "Liv's Temp Chart." She had become more and more obsessive about Liv's condition even though her status was fairly static. Yet Mel woke up 2 or 3 times in the night now, often from increasingly frequent nightmares, and walked down the hall to look in on a sleeping Liv.

Across the house, outside the study and beyond the small living room, the front door clicked and then swung open, thudding as it hit the doorstop. A thunk seconds later signaled that a backpack had dropped to the floor.

"Pick it up and put it where it belongs, Liv," Mel called. She clicked the "save" icon, rising from her chair at the same time.

"Hi, to you, too, Mom," Liv called. She picked up the backpack, slinging it over one shoulder.

Mel emerged from the study, arms extended. "Feel up to a driving lesson," Mel said as the two hugged.

"I don't think so. I probably should've skipped practice today. I'm exhausted." The backpack slipped off Liv's shoulder again, this time on to an end table.

"Watch out for the lamp, honey," Mel said. "Let's get a temperature check."

"Mom, I don't want to check my temperature. I'm just... like... tired." Liv dropped into an easy chair.

Mel went to the study and returned in a moment, putting the thermometer in her daughter's mouth. "Have you felt like this all day?" she asked.

With her lips closed around the end of the thermometer, Liv shook her head "no."

"What time did it start?"

Liv's eyes widened and she looked at Mel, pleading.

"You can answer. Show me your fingers."

Snorting in exasperation, Liv put up a single finger.

"One o'clock?" Mel confirmed.

Liv nodded.

"Dr. Resnick said occasional fevers aren't anything to worry about. We just need to keep track of them for trends."

" 'm not 'orried," she said, rolling her eyes.

Mel rubbed Liv's shoulder until the thermometer beeped. Liv instantly took it out. Mel snatched it.

"What's it say, Mom?" She tried to look around her mother's hand to read the temperature.

Mel pulled it away. "99.6. A little elevated, but no cause for concern." Mel did not feel that way. Incessant low level temps seemed more than just a reaction to the meds. She decided to call Doc Resnick again first thing in the morning to book another blood test.

CHAPTER 19

Freetown, Sierra Leone: Refugee Camp
November 12, 3:47 p.m. Greenwich Mean Time

The Karanjas' temporary tent had even smaller dimensions than the family's hut back in the village. With Jacob gone and Sara in the infirmary, the remaining three family members still ended up with more room individually.

Small comfort. Life would never be the same for them. A refugee camp was the last place Hamara wanted his people to end up. He had negotiated with the government for temporary housing in apartment buildings near the Waterloo section of the city by mid-November. The camp would be at most a three week stop for the Lokoma. Then, two days ago, Hamara met with the ministry's civilian administrator assigned to their case. There had been a last minute change, the man said. The apartment building had a snake infestation that had to be managed before anyone could move in. It would be at least another month before the Lokoma could leave the camp.

Then, yesterday, a suspicious Hamara visited the apartments in Waterloo and discovered that they had been occupied by cronies of the national leadership. This morning, he met again with the civilian administrator. The official assured the Chief that the apartments would no longer be necessary. The government would soon repatriate village lands to the Lokoma when the new bandit uprising in the bush ended. The military, he said, expected that would only be a matter of weeks. Hamara did not believe him. The President had just appointed one of the bandit leaders - who claimed legitimacy by calling himself a rebel - as a top aide.

In the press, Hamara read of the violence as a contest between political factions. He choked on rage when he read it. Rival gangs would be more like it. Organized crime of the worst kind. They fought over land suited for diamond and bauxite mining and other opportunities for exploitation. Cloaked in religions and ideologies, the "politicians" did not care about Christianity or Islam. They had no concept of either democracy or socialism. They only understood power and greed.

Day by day, it became more and more clear that the Freetown government had little more concern for Hamara's people than the bandits who raided his village. Hamara now even heard of tribes being forced out by the government to make room for corporate palm oil plantations.

De-humanizing living conditions in the camp made matters worse. The Catholic Church ran the camp, but the government made no effort to support the effort. Running water did not exist even though the government could make it available with a minor investment. Raw sewage, constantly filling the air with its odor, ran in narrow gutters carved out of the sandy loam of this section of Freetown. Bridged by wooden planks, the gutters carried the slop to fetid pools in the corners of the camp until rains could drive it to run off into bigger open sewers outside the camp. Yet too much rain could cause the gutters to spill over into the camp's narrow alleys, risking cholera and other disease.

"Nothing malicious," suggested one of the priests that managed the camp. "Just not a priority. The government's focused on its own survival."

Hamara chose to believe that it still bettered anarchy. At least with a government in place, order of some kind existed. Trucks with food and medicine did get through, something that did not happen readily in the bush. Instead, enormous bribes typically changed hands with criminal bands. The journey, Hamara heard, might entail many checkpoints manned by young boys like Jacob. The boys exacted a "toll" and the truck would pass with a somewhat lighter load. The same thing would happen at several other checkpoints, resulting in slim pickings by the time the medicines or food finally got to the original destination. Many relief agencies simply gave up on supplying the bush. Those few that still operated often participated in the corruption, diverting goods to well-to-do buyers.

Not that the food received in the urban refugee camps represented fine cuisine. Primarily composed of rice, beans and coffee, the foodstuffs lacked the green vegetables grown behind the village. Unlike home, meat never showed up at a table. Hamara had not wanted to leave the village. He wanted to stay and try to negotiate with the bandits, but the surviving elders thought it would be suicide. They had been fortunate to experience only a hit and run raid. They speculated that the rebels had been nervous about encountering nearby government troops if they remained for too long. Moreover, they had let most of the villagers survive, an indication that they planned to come back and use them for labor, possibly to exploit the bauxite deposits on tribal land just east of the village. Hamara did not believe that, though. The bauxite business in Sierra Leone had died in the early years of the civil war. Something else lie behind the raid. Probably something involving the aspirations of the Abo tribe and Fela, their chief who had partnered with a French company to build a small palm oil plantation elsewhere.

Hamara's priority concern remained Sara. She showed little improvement and needed constant medical attention. Taking her back to Lokoma was never a good option and the public clinic in Freetown would not keep her indefinitely. Had they not re-located, she would have been forced to continue to travel over an hour each way on bumpy roads, often slowed by dangerous checkpoints, just to visit a doctor. It proved to be the deciding factor that caused Hamara to concede to the thinking of the other elders. He quickly reached agreement with the government about the apartments in Waterloo and the temporary quarters in the refugee camp. In the process, he confirmed that the refugee camp had a central building with refrigeration capabilities for the blood vials Dave Clement had asked Hamara to collect for the malaria vaccine pilot program. After that, the trusting villagers packed up and convoyed in Red Cross trucks to the camp. Adrian Guerra had intervened to help secure the Red Cross assistance.

While accommodating Sara and providing medical options far superior to Lokoma, the camp's infirmary did not have up-to-date equipment, but the nurses, all Catholic nuns, mostly from other West African nations, had great bedside manner. Both pleasant and competent, they instilled confidence in the Karanjas. They had been the first to recognize that Sara had something other than malaria. Her immune system had all but collapsed; she suffered from a range of maladies, including thrush and sores that would not heal. It explained her chronic fever. Her body never had a chance to stop fighting its invaders.

Four days into their stay at the camp, Hamara and Mariama had met with Sara's doctor, a French physician, at the infirmary where Sara had been provided a bed and round the clock care. They visited Sara first. Small white beds filled the ward with narrow aisles between them. Children had their own ward separated from anyone over 15. Mariama gripped Hamara's arm tightly as they passed rows of children even more gaunt than Sara. Many lacked parts of arms or legs, maimed senselessly by machetes. They smiled at the children as they walked by them and, without exception, the children returned the smiles, some weakly but all genuinely.

Sara grinned and reached for her parents as they bent down at her bedside. She hugged them and whispered first in Hamara's ear and then Mariama's that she loved them. Even as bloodshot as they were, her eyes still gleamed and danced for her parents.

"Papa, you look worried," she said. "There's nothing to worry about. The medicine makes the pain go away."

"We want you to be all better and leave this place," Hamara said.

"I have friends here, Papa. They need our help."

"How can we help them?"

"Well…" Sara placed a finger on her mouth and thought. "Some need parents. Maybe we could take them with us when we go back to Lokoma."

"That might be a very good idea, sweet girl."

They talked animatedly for fifteen minutes. Sara seemed more concerned about the other children than herself. Then, it was time for their appointment.

"Don't go," Sara said as they started to walk away.

Both parents turned to see her big brown eyes wide and wet with tears.

"Papa, please lay down with me and tell me a story."

Heartache cut through the middle of Hamara. He bent over and hugged her, pressing her head into his shoulder. "I'll come back, little one. Tonight, I promise."

They started to walk away again. She called after them one more time. "Mama. Papa. Wait. Sing with me before you go."

"One verse," Mariama said tugging at Hamara's arm. "What song do you know?"

"The sisters taught me this one." She began singing, "Yes, Jesus loves me. Yes, Jesus loves me…"

Her parents held her hand quickly catching on to the words of the simple verse. When the song ended, Doctor Deauville appeared.

"I need them now, Sara," he said in English thick with a French accent. "I'll let them come back to you later."

In his small office, Deauville exchanged brief pleasantries and then proceeded to explore Sara's medical history in depth. There were no medical records for rural children in Sierra Leone and physicians typically had to rely on the memories of parents. He asked if Sara had ever had a transfusion and Hamara assured him she had not. Asked if she had ever used any dirty needles, Mariama explained that Sara had only been given injections by medical professionals.

The gray-haired doctor honed in further on this last question, tilting his reading glasses forward as he leaned close to a small wooden table to write. "So, these medical professionals, where were they?"

"They usually came to our village when some organization funded them. Over time, Sara received a measles shot, diphtheria and a tetanus shot."

"A tetanus shot? Did she get hurt?"

"She's always getting hurt. The medic that did it…"

"Not a doctor?"

"No. I don't think we ever had a real medical doctor visit our village."

The doctor's concern seemed to mount. "Did you observe how these medics used needles? Did they throw them away?"

"Usually. The tetanus fellow didn't though. I remember because I was impressed with how he economized. He re-used the needles, but only after dipping them in alcohol for fifteen seconds."

The doctor closed his eyes as if in silent prayer. Opening them, he took a hand each from Mariama and Hamara. "This medic - when did he come?"

"Two years ago, I think," Hamara spoke this time as Mariama bit her lip with concern.

"Did Sara get sick after he gave her the shot?"

"No, but she did a few weeks later," Mariama answered, "I remember that because until this time, it was the longest she had ever been down. She had no energy and ran fevers constantly for a few weeks."

"And she was fine until this current bout of malaria?"

"Yes," Hamara replied.

The doctor let go of their hands, rubbed his chin and then took his reading glasses off. "I'm going to need your permission to take blood from her."

"What are you looking for, doctor?" Mariama asked.

"I'm not certain, but it's not simply malaria."

"Then what?"

The doctor straightened up and squeezed their hands again. "It may be AIDS."

Twenty minutes later, the Karanjas exited the infirmary. They did not realize that the scope of a sniper's rifle held them in its crosshairs. The rifle peeked out from behind bushes atop one of the lush hills overlooking the camp.

Jacob saw his parents stop to talk with a nun in her white summer habit. He panned the camp with the scope, seeing more nuns and then a priest.

It's the Catholics, he thought. Just like the leaders said. He turned to the other boys. He nodded his head angrily. "It's like we were told. My father betrayed us to the Catholics. They want to destroy our way of life."

One of the boys spoke, "Then let's get them. Just like Rambo. We'll give them a message. And one day soon, Jacob, you will be paramount chief of Lokoma."

Jacob rubbed the irritating pocket cut into his temple. The rebel leaders administered his drugs through that pocket, medicines that gave him courage. Jacob thought they just made him angry.

"Why don't you fire?" the teenage commander demanded.

Jacob continued to peer through the scope, watching his parents walk through the camp below. His finger gently pressed on the trigger, but then let up. Then his father and mother disappeared into their makeshift home.

Suddenly, a kick between his shoulder blades knocked the wind out of Jacob. He looked up from the ground to see the commander.

"Why didn't you shoot?" the older boy demanded.

Jacob looked at him defiantly. "I'll shoot you instead," he responded.

"You'll die first."

First yanking the AK-47 out of Jacob's hands, the commander and two other teenagers pulled the ten year old up by his hair and the seat of his pants, throwing him down the trail.

"You don't deserve to carry a rifle!" one of them said.

"Move out, boy!" the commander ordered. "The rest of you, too. We're not done here."

Shortly after sunset, Jacob, now armed only with a machete, hid with the other boys amidst burned out cars near the back gate of the camp. They watched as three nuns left by the back gate of the camp and walked to their jeep. After a long day, they discussed looking forward to taking turns in a lukewarm bath, as good as it got, at the small motel room that acted as a convent.

The nun driving turned the ignition, but the jeep just made a grinding sound. "It always takes three tries," she said. "You think that they made it that way on purpose?"

The other nuns laughed as the driver turned the ignition again. The engine ground futilely for the second time. Jacob tensed, the drug-induced fuzziness in his head showing signs of clearing up. The boys around him hunched with machetes poised.

"Buckled up?" the driver asked. "We're going this time."

As predicted, the engine caught on the third try. The nun pushed the stick into first gear. It was too late. In the twilight, Jacob watched his comrades race quietly forward. In seconds, eight small, dark bodies hovered in silhouette over the nuns' white habits. Jacob stood back in violation of orders while the other boys stuffed rags in the women's mouths to muffle their screams as they dragged them from the jeep. The rebel leader selected the driver, pulled her roughly off to the side and tied her to the jeep's bumper.

Jacob fell to his knees, his own machete at his side as the boys went to work on the other two nuns whose horrified eyes bulged as they struggled to escape. The machetes had no mercy, chopping down first at the legs so they could not run. As the nuns flopped on the ground like beached fish, the boys clustered silently over them. The women stopped moving, whimpering, and praying Hail Marys in scream-like tones as the pain from their wounds caused them to convulse.

The leader noticed Jacob and glared at him. They were separated by the jeep. Jacob watched the older boy's eyes look down to his unbloodied machete. The leader turned away and gave a signal to the other boys. That started a mad kaleidoscope of swinging arms and flying blades. Jacob winced as the thudding blows of the machetes, their rusted metal whooshing as they sliced through the air, caught the women as they tried futilely to writhe out of range. Explosions of blood erupted mixed with small wooden rosary beads, now liberated from the chains that had enwrapped the waists of the mutilated Sisters. The boys did not stop as the women arched in death spasms, their bodies and their white habits transformed into a mash of blood and mud.

They then untied the remaining nun. She kicked and flailed, struggling to be heard through her gag. Four boys held her by the wrists and ankles as she tried to twist away. All of the others, except Jacob, huddled and flipped a coin several times. A boy emerged from the huddle. In a sudden movement, he hacked off the woman's left foot just above the ankle. Jacob heard her screams through the gag.

The leader hovered over the nun's face as she writhed in the hands of the boys with her three remaining limbs. "You've been spared to deliver a message," he said, nearly spitting at her. "But you won't have to say anything. Your body will speak for you."

He nodded at the other boys who bent over and held the thrashing woman down by the head and shoulders. One removed her gag and forced her mouth open while still another boy roughly sliced a knife through her tongue. She gurgled on her blood, as though struggling to get out a scream, but they shoved the gag back in her mouth before she could. Her slasher picked the bloody piece of tongue off the top of her habit, wiped it in the dirt, and stuffed the souvenir into his shorts.

"Go," said the leader and all but Jacob ran back up the hillside into the jungle.

Jacob defiantly walked past the leader toward the nun, his unused machete now lying in the dirt behind him. The leader slammed the butt of his machete handle into the crown of Jacob's head, knocking him to the ground.

"You're a coward, boy," the older boy said, waving the blade of his machete over Jacob's face. "If we didn't need you to get your father, you'd be dead."

Jacob stepped back up, but the leader shifted his attention to the nun. "Call them," the leader said to her as he yanked the gag out of her mouth.

He turned back toward Jacob and knocked him down again with a kick in the backside. Jacob started to reach for his machete, but the leader kicked it away. Jacob felt himself lifted by his tee shirt and he stumbled forward, kicked and shoved, as they headed back toward the hills. Behind him, he heard the nun gurgle and cough up blood.

Then, as he rounded the corner of the fence, he heard her begin to wail until her keening suffused the hillside and the camp.

CHAPTER 20

Liv's Diary
November 13, 10:12 p.m. Mountain Time

One day. One day makes all the difference in the world. Michael Winston talked to me in history. THE Michael Winston. He had no reason to talk. He just did it. Yesterday, he did not know I even existed. He asked me about volleyball. He said he thought it was VERY cool that I played.

I haven't felt this way about a boy since... forever. I better figure out how to beat this stupid disease. There's someone really hot to live for. It is ALSO absolutely essential that I figure out the kissing rules for HIV. I'm pretty sure there aren't any, but there is no way I will take a chance with his life. What if I can't kiss him? No. That would not be acceptable. I can only imagine what it would be like if he kissed me. If I can never kiss him, I'll never forgive her. It had to be her and her slutty behavior. I need to tell her before she hurts someone else. If it is her. But what if it's not? What if she gets pissed off and tells the whole school? I don't know how I would deal with that. Better to think about what it would be like to kiss Michael, how I'd feel inside – how I feel right now. Oh wow.

Can't go there. Even diaries can't hear some things. Especially if parents ever read them. Which you'd better not be doing. If you are, close this RIGHT NOW, Mother.

CHAPTER 21

Loveland, Prodeus headquarters
November 14, 4:48 p.m., Mountain Time

Outside Dave's office window, the setting sun melted into puffy clouds on the western horizon, casting a soft pink light on Colorado's Front Range. Glancing at it over his shoulder, Dave caught his afternoon beard on the collar of his pale blue dress shirt. He quickly re-focused his attention on the thick bundle of paper in his hand, unconsciously rubbing the new tender spot on his jaw.

He searched the pages for bad news, anything that said the PDNA would or should be further delayed. But the engineering verification test (EVT) results, the outcome of eight weeks of intense testing, said otherwise on the pages before him. The PDNA could be deployed right on schedule, pending the results of beta tests now ongoing at the Aldrich. His undivided attention the last few weeks had paid dividends on making the nearly impossible happen. Trips to Geneva, New York and Washington, DC, had already bridged several of the key relationship gaps caused by Evan Conger's unexpected demise. But the biggest gap for him remained the complete absence of contact with Sheila Stratemeier. She offered hope for Liv and then completely cut off communication. He checked her cloud repository several times a day, but no new documents had arrived. He thought about calling her at the lab under some pretense, but knew Aldrich security would be eavesdropping. If her got her fired, that would not be good for either one of them. He decided to give her another ten days. Sheila was clever; she would eventually find a way to get around security.

Looking at his phone, he saw that it was 4:56. Liv's game started in nineteen minutes. He could be there in 25. There would be no traffic at this hour. He would only miss a few minutes. He drummed his fingers on the desk and then grabbed a pen. He ran the pen down a checklist from the signed-off product definition document. All the function was there. Brian Middleton would argue that he should not have been surprised, but lately Middleton had not impressed him as the sharpest engineering VP. Nonetheless, Brian had rallied his team and it looked like he had brought in the result.

Jennifer tapped at the door, interrupting his thoughts.

"I was wondering if you were going to show up. You're going to make me late for volleyball again," Dave said. He glanced at his phone. 4:59.

Jennifer sat, folded her hands atop her short black lace skirt, her knees parted slightly. She looked beyond Dave to the horizon. The last gasp of twilight silhouetted her in shades of pink and gray, making her features difficult to discern for Dave.

"What a gorgeous sky!"

Dave did not look. "It's beautiful. So what's the word?"

"Beta's progressing well."

"Did you read the EVT?"

"Every page as the team put it together."

"Any issues with the beta?"

"No. So far everything supports the EVT. No major surprises. Couple of small modifications, but we made them on the spot."

"Were they factored in EVT?"

"We put them in."

Dave sat back, laying the checklist on his desk and moving the bulky test document to the side. He had a digital copy to reference as well, but found reviewing a printed version made him less likely to miss details. "Congratulations, Jenn. You've done a good job. Middleton gave you exactly what we wanted."

Visibly relaxing, Jennifer crossed her legs and interlaced her hands over her knee. "Thanks. You're a wonderful mentor."

"I want a press release," he said.

"About your mentorship?" she quizzed, clearly an attempt at humor.

"Very funny. We want Claire to agree to a joint release that tells the world this is working. That should help with funding and maybe even flush out a few new sales prospects."

Another glance at his phone. 5:04. Twilight no longer suffused the room, only the overhead fluorescents, as darkness settled in outside.

"Boy, you're all business," Jennifer said, sitting upright in the chair, her forearms planted firmly on the armrests.

Dave stood and reached for his briefcase, but Jennifer remained in her seat.

"How's the rock climber?" she asked.

"Waiting for me to show up at her game right now," he said. He reached his door and held out an arm to show Jennifer out.

"So is Mel still too busy to find time for lunch with you?"

"She's busy," Dave said, immediately knowing he had made a mistake to even acknowledge the question. Seeing Jennifer was not moving, he turned off the light. "Sorry, I need to go," he said.

Jennifer sat in the dark, unmoving. Dave stood still at the door, not knowing what to do next.

"Dave," she said, finally rising from her seat. "Would you be offended if I told you that you were very attractive, very sexy?"

"Don't do this." Dave turned to go out the door, but Jennifer deftly placed a hand on his shoulder and turned him. She quickly weaved her arms under his, placing one hand behind the nape of his neck and another in the center of his back. Pushing up from her toes, she pulled him to her and planted soft, moist lips on his. He tasted her lip-gloss and smelled the musk of her perfume. He felt her tongue part his lips. His mouth, half open in astonishment, received her without immediate resistance. He felt himself becoming aroused, but anger erupted almost simultaneously.

"What are you doing?" he whispered, pulling away.

She put a finger to her lips. "Shhh. You don't want anyone to hear us."

Dave held his arms out at his side and stepped back. "Jenn, this is a very bad idea." He exited the office and moved toward the stairs that led to the building's lobby.

"You can't tell me you don't like me," she persisted as she followed him to the top of the stairs.

"Not that way." He held up his phone. 5:09. "I have to go. I can't miss this game." He turned and raced down the stairs.

"No goodbye?" Jennifer called as he took the steps two at a time.

CHAPTER 22

Fort Collins High School, Gym
November 14, 5:43 p.m. Mountain Time

Liv wiped the sweat from her forehead. She loved volleyball, but tonight she only wished the game would end. The nausea had begun to feel too compelling. She hated feeling sick; she feared she would embarrass herself in front of everyone, including the boys in the bleachers. Tonight, all the calls and cheers from the stands collapsed into a persistent dissonance that throbbed inside her head. Of all the nights, she could not believe that Michael had chosen tonight to come to his first volleyball game. There was a very good chance he would get to see her barf.

He kept smiling at her all day. Every time he saw her. Now, her body desperately wanted to ruin her love buzz. She could not believe how badly she wanted him to leave the gym.

She looked at the scoreboard: 14-13. If they got this point, Fort Collins would win. Game over.

Liv took a shivering breath. She poised to jump as Chelsea served a hard line drive into the far left corner of Poudre Valley's court. One of the Poudre Valley girls leapt parallel to the floor, sending a spike soaring back – right to where Liv did not want it to go. Right at her.

"Oh, please," cried Liv as she leapt to the side and flung her right arm at the inbound ball.

"Aiii," she yelled as she brought her fist around, hitting the ball with the inside of her right wrist. It ricocheted off her own head. She crumpled to the ground, her vision half gone, as the ball bounced free at her feet.

Her teammates immediately came to her.

"Liv, are you all right?"

"Liv?"

"Don't move, Liv. We'll get help."

She managed to force out, "I'm okay."

"All right," one of the girls said.

"Tough break," encouraged another. "You were fast, but there was no way to save that one."

Chelsea and two others pulled Liv back to her feet. "Way to sacrifice the body," Chelsea encouraged.

Liv started to vomit, but choked back the reflex.

On the opponents' side of the net, a PVH girl prepared to serve the ball. From the sideline, the coach tried to get Liv's attention. He gave her a thumbs-up, the concerned look on his face forming into a question. She acknowledged him with a thumbs-up and focused on the server. Her team could have finished the game with that last point, but her miscue had kept them on the court.

The ball soared over the net into Fort Collins' back line. There, Chelsea popped a perfect set-up to the front row where Alyssa prepared to slam it. Instead, PVH's tallest player timed a jump perfectly and bounced the kill shot right back at Alyssa. The ball bounced off the net and hit the ground. The partisan crowd groaned audibly.

14-14. Now Ft. Collins would need two more points to win.

"That's all right, Alyssa," one of the girls called. "Let's get her back right now!"

"Next set-up's coming your way, Liv," Chelsea yelled from the corner. "C'mon, you guys, let's get the serve back."

The serve sailed over the net and looked long. Chelsea and another girl in the back row stepped aside to let it land. It looked like a good decision. The ball landed just outside the line, making it a PVH foul.

The ref did not see it that way. She insisted the ball had landed inbounds.

"Are you out of your mind?" Chelsea shouted. "That ball was…"

Liv ran back to her friend and put a hand on her mouth. "You'll get thrown out," Liv said between gritted teeth. "We need you."

Chelsea balled her hands into fists, closed her eyes and blew out. "You're right. You're right. Let's just get 'em."

Liv nodded, but as she did, her head started swimming.

"Game point," the ref called. "14-15."

Liv wobbled back to her position, wondering if she should have the coach pull her. It was too late. The next serve floated lazily over the net toward the backcourt. A perfect set-up. Chelsea ran under it and deftly popped it high into the air, bringing its trajectory right down on top of Liv.

Looking up, Liv positioned under the ball. Her dizziness caused her to stumble back, but as the ball came down, she moved back into position. A wide gap opened on the PVH side of the court. Liv leapt into the air, ready to slam a spike into the gap. Her right arm made a wide arc and whipped around and into the ball. Perfect form. Perfect timing. Except that she barely tipped it as her head swooned. The ball dropped to the floor behind her. Liv collapsed beside it, bouncing her left shoulder off the floor.

"Clement!" Chelsea yelled in disbelief. They had lost the game.

The gym was completely silent except for a handful of whoops from the PVH players as the Fort Collins team began dejectedly walking off the court, the coach waving them into a huddle on the sideline. Mel stood frozen in the stands. Liv still lay on the floor. She did not move.

Stepping awkwardly down the bleachers, Mel kept her eye on Liv and began yelling, "Coach! Coach! Coach Stefanik!"

The coach looked up toward the bleachers. Seeing Mel coming, he looked for Liv, seeing her motionless on the floor. He pushed past the inbound team, quickly dropping to one knee beside Liv. Seconds later, Mel joined him.

Stefanik gently rolled Liv on to her back. The PVH team noticed what was happening and turned their attention back to the court. Soon, the Fort Collins team also saw Liv down. Within thirty seconds, the entire gym focused its attention on the drama being played out on the floor of the court.

"Get me a towel," the coach called back to his bench.

Three of the girls were quickly at his side with towels. He took one and rolled it up under Liv's neck. He put the other two beneath her knees in order to elevate her legs. Soon, several doctors, parents of Liv's teammates, showed up at the side of the coach and Mel. The others quickly deferred to Bill Ralides, a trauma specialist who ran the emergency room at Poudre Valley Hospital. Bill had already called for an ambulance on his cell phone.

He put a hand on each side of her face and watched her closed eyes. "What's her name?" he asked.

"Liv Clement," Mel replied.

"Liv!" he called. "Liv, do you hear me?"

She did not respond. He checked her pulse. After placing a hand on her forehead, he felt the thick swell of inflamed glands beneath her jaw. Mel dropped to her knees beside the doctor. She mumbled a prayer as her fingernails clawed into her palms.

"Coach, have someone get a damp towel or washcloth over here," Ralides said.

"I've got it, coach," said Chelsea who had been standing over the doctor watching.

Across the gym, Dave raced through the door, his excuse for tonight circling his brain in anticipation of being with Mel and Liv for the first time in a week. Seeing the crowd on the floor, he assumed the game had just ended.

"Dammit," he mumbled. He scanned the crowd for Mel, but could not see her. Everyone seemed to be clustering on the other side of the net. Must be a post-game prayer, he thought.

He looked up to the scoreboard and saw the bad news. Moving toward the cluster, he continued to look for Mel. Behind him at the door, he heard the whoop of a siren. Turning, he saw blue uniformed paramedics come running in. Panic surged inside him.

A path cleared for the paramedics. For the first time, Dave saw Mel. She knelt on the court, holding a prone Liv's hand. A whispered plea burst from Dave's lips, "God, no!"

The paramedics asked Mel to step back. Dave came up and latched on to her arm.

"What happened?" he asked.

Between gritted teeth, Mel whispered, "She passed out. Where the hell were you?"

"I'm sorry. This business…" He stopped himself, his prepared excuse now seeming absurd. "I screwed up," he said. "I should have been here."

She stared at him, her mouth half open as tears welled out of her eyes. "Thank you for finally giving me a straight answer," she said as she choked up even more.

Dave hugged her. She placed the side of her face against his shoulder and sobbed. "I am so sorry," he said as they watched the paramedics go to work.

CHAPTER 23

Fort Collins, Poudre Valley Hospital Emergency Room
November 14, 6:27 p.m. Mountain Time

As Dave drove behind the ambulance containing Liv and Mel, the trees of the orderly streets of Fort Collins hovered above, providing a hunkering, eerie corridor that intermittently burst into orange, yellow or red as occasional street lights illuminated the rusting late autumn leaves. As the ambulance crossed LeMay Avenue, it briefly flashed its lights and sounded its siren.

At the emergency room door, the paramedics opened the rear doors of the ambulance. Dave parked, running over just as they transported Liv to a gurney under the white halogen lights of the porte cochere. He lightened immediately when he encountered a smiling Liv with eyes bleary but open. With Dave and Mel holding one of Liv's hands on each side of the gurney, the paramedics rolled her over the entry's marble floor to a treatment room behind the automatic doors where they transferred her to a bed.

"Did I get it over?" Liv asked.

"What, sweetheart?" Mel responded.

"The ball, mom. Did I get it over the net? Did we get the point?"

"That is not what's important right now."

"Oh, no," Liv said, closing her eyes as her mother's response made the answer obvious. "Did we lose?"

Dave squeezed her hand. "What matters right now is your health," he said.

"They must hate me."

Mel leaned down and kissed her forehead. "No one hates you," she said. "They're worried about you, not volleyball. There's plenty of season ahead."

"I'm so embarrassed," Liv said through half-closed eyes.

"There's nothing to be embarrassed about," Dave said.

Liv rolled her eyes. "Mom, what will we tell people? Another dehydration story?"

"If we have to," Mel responded.

"Perfect. I black out from dehydration at exactly the right moment to lose the game."

"They'll just think you took a payoff from the other team," Dave said.

A small chuckle popped out of Liv. Mel gently stroked her forehead.

"You feel hot," Mel said.

"Does your head hurt?" Dave asked.

"No, I'm just tired right now. And maybe a little hungry."

Thinking about ordering a pizza, Dave reached for his cell phone. And panicked. His phone was not in the holster on his belt.

"What's wrong?" Mel asked.

"Daddy, are you okay?"

"No, I'm not," he said evenly, trying to control his anxiety. "My phone's missing."

Mel grabbed his arm and glared at him. "No way are you doing this now," she whispered between gritted teeth.

"You sure you brought it in?" Liv asked.

"I'm not sure of anything. I'll be back in a minute."

As he hurried to the parking lot, Dave tried to remember when he had last seen or used the phone. Normally, he constantly stayed on it while in the car. But tonight he had not even picked it up, not even thought about it. For a short while, he had actually left the office behind as he focused on Liv.

He climbed into the driver's seat and turned on the overhead light. His phone sat on the center console, an alert on the screen indicating he had voice mails. He started to listen to the voicemails when he saw Paul Resnick go through the emergency room doors. He finished one last voicemail and then followed the doctor inside.

As he entered the examination area of the emergency room, he saw Paul take Mel by the arm and escort her out of the bay where Liv now slept. Seeing Dave coming, Mel turned and waited while the doctor disappeared down the hall.

"Did you find your phone? Mel asked.

He showed it to her.

"You should have it attached permanently while we're here."

"Funny," he said.

"Liv's idea."

Resnick returned quickly and led them to a private exam room. He climbed on to the edge of the exam table while Mel and Dave took the chairs.

"Liv's blood test came back yesterday," he said. "I hadn't had a chance to look at them. Until I got the call tonight. I'm sorry I didn't review them sooner."

"What were the results, Paul?" Mel asked.

"Her CD4 T-cell count is down," Resnick said.

"How far?" Dave asked.

"Down to 375. Not dangerous, but that's a decline of over 150 in a month. Could mean her viral load is up, too, which would explain the weakness."

Mel folded her hands in her lap, squeezing them tightly. "That's a fast drop," she said.

"Could she be skipping doses, Mel?" Dave asked.

Mel set her jaw. "She's taking her meds. Paul knows about the couple of skipped doses."

"A few skipped doses probably would not result in this big an impact," Resnick said. "I'm not too concerned because her CD4 ratio to total lymphocytes is at 29%, down only slightly from six weeks ago when it was 31%."

"How do we reverse the trend?" Mel asked.

"I don't know if it's a trend, Mel. CD4 count and ratio can fluctuate over the course of a day in a completely healthy individual. But Liv's fever and her passing out at the game are reasons for concern."

"So what do we do?"

"I think we just keep monitoring her closely. The disappointing thing here is that she's not showing sustainable improvement with the drug regimen she's on. It may be that she's simply been overdoing it. Wouldn't hurt for her to slow down a little bit and see where things go."

"I should have kept her out of practice," Mel said. "The tiredness and dizziness. The low-grade fevers. I should have stepped in."

Dave leaned forward in his seat. "You've known about this?" he asked. "What the hell, Mel?"

"A fever, that's all, Dave. She's run chronic fevers off and on since her first period."

"There's no blame to place here," the doctor said. "Liv may have even caught a virus. Her immune system is still strong enough to fight most things off. This event tonight could even be a by-product of the medications. They're pretty strong and take a toll of their own."

Dave looked at Mel. He knew he had been out of line. He reached for her hand. She let him take it, but did not look at him. He helped her to her feet.

They were all standing now, very close to each other between the exam table and the closed door. Dave, a broad-shouldered six-footer, dwarfed the short, lean doctor, who was barely Mel's height.

"Should we be thinking about a change in medication?" Dave asked.

"I'll consult with Lisa Ellis, but I think it's too soon to make that call." Resnick relied on Dr. Ellis, the infectious disease specialist, for consults on Liv's case. He sent Liv to Dr. Ellis for the original diagnosis in the summer. "Her body isn't responding to the current regimen as well as I'd like, but that could just be a normal fluctuation. Let's see where she is on the next test. I'll want to do that again in a few weeks after she's rested up.'."

"Be brutally honest with us, Paul," he said. "Should we be concerned?"

"Of course," he said. "It's HIV. You have to be vigilant."

In the corridor, Dave could tell Mel was restraining herself from erupting at him. He whispered to her, "I'm sorry I jumped on you in there. This thing has me feeling completely without control."

"Welcome to the club."

"I need to move back in."

"So you're done saving the world? Should've thought of that before you opened your mouth in there."

"I can help."

"Do what? Make sure I'm monitoring her drugs properly? I'll manage."

"I admitted I was out of line. When it comes to Liv, I defend and I attack. I don't think very clearly."

"If you want to help her, come through on the so-called cure you promised her."

"I'm working on it. I swear to God. I think of it constantly."

Arms folded, she scrutinized him. "You jumped the gun, didn't you?"

"No. No I didn't. The Aldrich threw up a tighter security net when Evan died. We have to breach that net to get to the answer. It will happen. Just not as soon as we hoped."

She continued to contemplate him. He knew she was probably looking at the first sign of jowls on his jaw, the waist threatening to spill over the top of the belt, the gray on the temples. He hoped she saw the sincere appeal in his eyes, not the ambition and bluster to which he had too often succumbed over the years. She had told him she hated that most of all because it hid the innocent dreamer with whom she fell in love, the up-from-nothing young man who catered to her and hung on her every word, a can-do optimist who would never let the world overwhelm either one of them, a man who knew how to get what his family needed.

A tiny smile appeared on her face. She squeezed her eyes shut to blink back tears.

Dave took her hands. He pulled her close. They hugged for only the second time since he returned from the aborted Geneva trip. She buried her face in his neck. He placed one hand in her hair behind her head, the other on her back, gently pulling her even closer.

"You're warm," he said. "I miss this."

She pulled away from him. She wiped away a tear. "Too soon," she whispered as she started walking toward the bay where Liv waited.

CHAPTER 24

Sierra Leone, Rebel CAMP
November 17, 9:10 p.m. Greenwich Mean Time

Ani Karanja lay naked on the damp earth. Warm drops of water fell erratically from the jungle canopy, smearing the mud caked on her skin. Bruised and bleeding in countless places, she smelled of the men who had repeatedly raped her. Sometimes they came alone, sometimes in groups of two, three or four. The groups were the worst, using every available part of her body at the same time, bouncing on her as though she were a human trampoline, often striking her with cartridge belts while they played.

She touched her lower back, gingerly feeling the bruised, painful ridges that dented her skin with the outline of the cartridges. Putting her hands on her face, she tried to squeeze out tears that would no longer come. She looked at her fingernails, growing back but still bent and broken from the first rapes when she still fought back, still dug her nails into these boys, shocked that nothing discouraged their drug-induced aggression, not her nails, not her teeth, not a well-placed knee.

The rebel leader, a boy several years younger than her, called her his wife now. He said he liked her spirit, that he wanted to own the wife of a chief. Thus far, that had spared her the physical mutilations others had experienced. She mumbled prayers constantly, but never in front of her captors. They had warned the captives against praying. They had said they did not know what spirits the women might invoke, making prayer an execution offense.

She listened to their conversations, trying to make sense of what they were doing. All she heard about were drugs, drink, sex and payment. They seemed to be focused primarily on looting and killing. Few of them were older than their teens. They had the limited and childish vocabulary of elementary school children, exactly what they probably were when first kidnapped into this life. Blood thirst filled them, quenched at whim, particularly when they were drunk or high.

Ani had befriended a young pregnant girl, only to watch her dragged into a clearing and disemboweled, the baby and her organs, glistening with blood and mucus, tumbling on to her belly and the ground. Screaming, the girl called on God to curse them as they began their torture. One of them grabbed her by the hair and held her by the neck as another swiftly cut out her tongue with a crude knife. They left her to slowly bleed to death on the ground, crying out incoherently as she held on to the small, dead baby still attached to her by its deteriorating umbilical cord.

Soon, Ani only wanted to die, to escape her body. She hated her captors, but would not speak out against them for fear of losing her own tongue. She grasped hope in prayer, praying in her head, praying to any version of God that would listen, hoping that the kind God that Hamara served would prevail in the end. Too many harsh gods already filled the land. At first, she could not pray while they used her, too ashamed, but she remembered that the Christian God healed lepers, the lowest of the people in his time. He taught his followers to forgive, to always forgive. He would forgive her, this God who had broken her family. He owed her. She struggled with her side of that equation, struggled to forgive this allegedly good God and these demons who tossed her around like a rag doll.

At night, she and two other wives would cook for the rebel leader who called himself husband to the three of them. He would invite other soldiers to join him, bragging how his "wives" were there to serve all of them. Every night, they drank and used drugs. Sometimes, they were so caught up in telling each other stories that they passed out before they got to the women. Other nights, the women would be pulled into the midst of them and made to do sexual favors.

Tonight, she had been discarded early. Her abdomen screamed at her, every muscle in it spasming from the evening's ordeal. Her gag reflex never seemed to stop. But she had so little to eat that little more than spit and the effluvium of her captors came out.

Lying in the trees, trying not to groan and draw attention, she listened to them brag to each other of how they were using the villagers' own children to go back and do the killing.

"This one killed your father," they would tell the little boys. "These people are the killer's family. You must avenge your father."

And nine and ten year olds would go into villages hacking people to death as instructed.

So at night, these teenagers would brag of these manipulations and mutilations. They took great delight in the blood they shed. Ani struggled to find something, but could find nothing redeemable about these children with whom she was doomed to spend her life or die. Ani and the other women prepared the meals for the boys who grew in number with each attack. Into every pot of gruel, they sprinkled gunpowder as instructed. The leaders said it would make the boys strong – and crazy.

Under a tree in the mud, she crawled to some undergrowth and pulled down leaves and grass to cover herself. She prayed for Jacob. He had been missing when she was kidnapped. Hopefully, he had run to safety. But she knew young boys did not get to wander the jungle alone for long. They would be murdered or quickly impressed into one of the bandit groups as soldiers. As she had been dragged through the rainforest, she had witnessed boys, some younger than Jacob, mutilate and kill people, sometimes whole families, egged on by the young men who led them. There seemed to be no purpose to it other than looting and sadism.

If he has been captured, will he become like one of these? she wondered.

Jacob, the faithful boy, the sensitive boy. Will he end up an animal like them? Would that be better or worse than were they to kill him? Worse, she thought. Much worse. She almost started to pray for his death, but latched on to a small hope that some other fate had befallen him, something that had returned him to the safety of Hamara.

Hearing footsteps in the brush, she slid closer to the tree, hoping that she would not be noticed in the darkness.

CHAPTER 25

Fort Collins High School, Choir Room
November 18, 10:53 a.m. Mountain Time

Liv watched attentively as Beth McKelvey thrust her hands forward and then up. A last blast of imperfect harmony erupted within the choir room.

"Better," said McKelvey. She closed the music on the stand before her. "Tryouts start tomorrow during class so bring something to study while you wait." The teacher shoved the music in a folder and turned toward the door, signaling the end of class. Noise exploded from the rehearsal room's silence as chairs banged into chairs, squeaking on the wooden floor and plywood risers. Students called and chattered at each other, aiming their voices in multiple directions over both short and long distances.

"Clement," called Chelsea, weaving through bodies as she descended the risers. "Wait up, Liv!"

Liv, a second soprano, stood by her seat on the front row at the bottom of the risers, sparing her the foot traffic Chelsea encountered. Holding her books to her chest, she nodded in acknowledgement. Singing made her feel good. She closed her eyes and bobbed her head, quietly singing the last song to herself, enjoying a moment of what had become very precious peace.

"Liv!" The voice came from a new direction. It was Ellen Melby.

"Hi, Ellen."

"Did you quit volleyball?"

Liv's face reddened. "No. Who told you that?"

"Like everyone. You've missed three days of school and you haven't been at practice since you got hurt."

"I haven't quit, Ellen," Liv said.

"Good. I never thought of you as a quitter."

Frustration and discouragement welled up in Liv. She wanted to blurt out that she was sick, very damned sick with a disease only gays and whores got – to demand an explanation for God's extreme sanction. Instead, she stared. Mom said to think "smile" when the blows came. Smile and make like a great actress.

"Dehydration," she said, certain Ellen could see the phoniness in her grin, sense the flimsiness of her tale.

"Dehydration?" Ellen asked, "Liv, nobody misses a week of practice because of dehydration."

Liv's smile crinkled. She felt her mouth muscles quiver as she fought the urge to cry, torn between shame and anger.

A gentle hand landed on the side of her waist, relaxing her face instantly. Chelsea now stood at her side. "Did you ever have it, Melby?" Chelsea asked.

"No," Ellen responded, her voice indignant.

"Then how would you know?"

"Common sense."

"Since when did you get any of that?"

"Harsh, Chelsea. I'm just worried about the truth."

"That doesn't even deserve an answer. Maybe you ought to take a course on being a real friend."

Ellen shook her head and walked off.

"Thanks, Chels," Liv said

"No problem."

"I'm sorry I put you in the middle. She's going to hate you now."

"She was mean to you."

"I can deal with it." Liv clipped her words, as though shorter words might better mask her shame.

"Did I upset you by stepping in?"

"I'm not upset. I just feel bad that I came between you guys."

"Ellen and I aren't lesbos or anything. It's no big deal. Anyway, you seem like you need a little more help than usual lately."

They walked out into the corridor. Liv wondered if she should say something now. Chelsea needed to know. She needed Chelsea to know. But not here. Not now.

"It's the dehydration," Liv said. "It wore me down. My doctor says it can take weeks to get back to normal. Affects your muscles and your brain."

Chelsea stopped and stepped toward the lockers to get out of traffic. "Listen, Liv. I'm your friend. Something's wrong and it's not dehydration."

Liv suppressed a four letter word. She knows, Liv thought. Because she has inside information on this.

Chelsea continued, "But you're my friend no matter what."

Liv felt a burden start to lift. Everything finally could come out in the open Chelsea. "Why didn't you tell - " Liv started, but Chelsea interrupted.

"You can tell me what it really is. I know you're not pregnant. You're just not capable of that. We can rule out an STD, too."

Liv's heart dropped. Chelsea either really did not know or she was in denial. They started walking again and Chelsea started to put an affectionate arm on Liv's shoulder. "Liv, stop," Chelsea whispered suddenly. Pushing Liv with her, she turned toward the lockers.

"What are you doing?"

"He's looking over here."

Liv turned her head to see Michael Winston peering over shorter students. She smiled. He smiled back.

"I'm asking him out," Chelsea said.

"What about Aidan?"

"Yesterday's news."

Liv turned toward her friend with a stunned look. "Why do you think

Michael will go out with you?"

"He looks at me all the time."

Because you're my friend, Liv thought. "He could be looking at me, too."

"Don't get any ideas, Clement. I have a claim on this guy."

Liv wanted to argue, but she felt light-headed again, her signal to find a place to sit. "I have to go to the library," Liv said. "We should finish this later."

"I thought we were going to decide which parts to go for."

"Parts?"

"The musical, Ms. Alzheimers."

"I'm…" Liv knew she probably would not be well enough to be in the musical. It seemed so unfair. She wondered why Chelsea remained healthy. She had been as much a part of it. And if she was the source, she was at least a carrier, a danger to anyone with whom she was intimate. Liv felt herself growing angry. "You can't do this to him," she said.

"To Michael? Do what?"

"You know what."

"Like I really have no clue, Clement."

Liv stepped closer, her face just a few inches from Chelsea's.

"What?" Chelsea said.

Liv took a deep breath and shivered. She stepped back. "We need to talk, but not now," she said as she started walking away. "I have to go."

"Clement, what is up with you?" Chelsea called.

Liv walked faster, turning toward the library.

CHAPTER 26

Prodeus Offices
November 18, 11:10 a.m.

Pushing his chair away from his desk, Dave grabbed his coffee mug. He pulled a Celestial Seasonings Tension Tamer teabag out of the center desk drawer and headed for the hallway outside where he would find both the network printer and hot water. As he pushed the handle for the hot water, he thought of just how hard Fort Collins might run from Liv if word leaked out. If her symptoms became visible, people would know something was up.

Walking back toward his office, he banged into Jennifer as she hurried around a corner.

"Great," she said. "Just who I wanted to see. Got a minute?"

Dave hesitated. He wanted to read some more, maybe get back on the web.

"Sure," he finally said.

In his office, Jennifer dropped a two-page report on his desk.

"This is it, boss. Page one summarizes the prototype testing at the Aldrich. The PDNA works like a champ."

"Finally," Dave said as he began to turn to the second page.

Jennifer slammed her hand down on the paper. "Be patient," she said. "Let me tell you first."

He stood motionless, slightly startled. "Okay. Tell me."

"The second page is Aldrich engineering's authorization to fulfill the 400 unit PO."

A rush of triumph surged through Dave. He put his hand up for a high five. Jennifer grasped his hand instead, pulling him to her for a tight hug. Leaning back, she grabbed his jaw with her free hand and pulled him to her for a kiss.

"No, Jenn," he said as he tried to back away, but her hand squeezed tighter around his jaw instead.

She dropped one hand and grabbed his belt, pulling him still closer, her lips softly caressing his while her tongue probed his unprepared mouth. Dave did not want to hurt her. He knew that no one would believe his side of the story. So he bit down hard on her tongue.

"Ouch!" she shrieked. "What the hell?"

"I said no, Jennifer, and I meant no." He walked around his desk and sat down.

She touched her tongue and then looked at her finger. "No blood," she said. "I might have liked that under other circumstances. Still, it started out nice." Her cheeks flushed. She fanned her face with her hand as she sat down. "A little warm in here."

He grunted.

"You're blushing, boss," she said.

His mouth had the texture of cotton. Words barely struggled out. "We need to talk about this. I have a family and a good marriage. There is nothing else I need in that category."

"You didn't say you loved your wife, the one that threw you out of the house."

"I do love her."

"Now you did. After I prompted you."

He wiped a hand across his brow.

"I can be discrete," she said. "What happens at the office stays at the office."

"Stop. I can't keep you around if you keep this up."

Leaning forward in her chair, hands on her thighs, knees slightly askew, she held his eyes, the glimmering emerald of her own eyes both alluring and sinister to Dave. She seemed excited by his discomfort.

"You won't fire me. You and I both know that. You need me around here."

"Not that badly."

"Oh, c'mon, Dave. What about Claire? What about the Aldrich development team? You want to give that to Middleton and his reverse engineering squad?"

He shifted in his chair. A glance drew his eyes to the long smooth arc of flesh above her knee as her slender thigh disappeared under her skirt. He looked away. He definitely needed to move back home.

"Listen, Jenn. I like you. We've grown close on this project, but it's not romance. If you can leave that behind, there's a friendship and working relationship we can salvage."

"How about lust then?" She squeezed her hands together between her knees.

He glared at her in alarm. "Jenn -"

"Take life where you meet it, Dave. Denial is never a good thing."

His face reddened. His hormones hinted they might take charge and veto common sense. Too many long months away from home, he thought. He pressed the speaker button on his phone and dialed Anne's extension..

"Yes," Anne answered.

"Can you come in for a minute?" he asked.

"Coward," Jennifer whispered, her eyes narrowed above a knowing smile. Anne entered.

"We need copies of this for Ed and the rest of the executive staff." He handed her the Aldrich order, waiting for a reaction. She took it and studied it briefly.

"Yes!" she shouted, jumping once in place. "Congratulations, boss."

"Congratulations to all of us," he said. "This team, including you both, has worked damned hard to get to this point."

"Should I put together an e-mail over your signature saying that?"

"I appreciate the offer, but that's something I need to do myself."

"Understand." Anne left the room.

"Nicely done," Jennifer said. "Masterful change of subject."

"I have to get some work done. I'll see you later at the production meeting."

As Jennifer stood, Dave watched her eyes land on the AIDS book hiding behind the computer monitor. "You have something else you want to tell me?" she asked.

Dave placed a yellow pad over the book to hide it.

"I saw the title, Dave," she said.

"I don't have AIDS if that's what you mean."

"You know, that's one of the benefits of my Aldrich contacts."

"How's that?"

She started to circle the desk toward him. "Well, if you get AIDS, they're very close to a cure. I'll just get you right to the head of the line. That way, you're covered if a promiscuous little girl like me gives you a bad disease."

Dave's eyes zeroed in on her. "You're lying."

"Why would I lie to you, Dave?" she asked.

She drew closer. He placed a hand on her shoulder and gently pushed her back. "I've talked to Claire," he said. "There is no HIV work. The Aldrich is focused almost exclusively on malaria."

Jennifer knitted her eyebrows. "I'm not lying, Dave. And I'm not stupid. If you really do have it, you should tell me. Is that why Mel threw you out? Or did she give it to you? That bitch."

Dave quickly shook his head. "She's not a bitch."

"Really?"

"Really. And neither one of us are sick.

"So why the interest in the Aldrich work?"

"You brought up AIDS."

Jennifer rolled her eyes. "I brought it up?" she said. "You're the one hiding a book about it."

"Jenn, if you know something, you need to let me know."

"I can't," Jennifer spoke, her face sincere. "Not in good conscience. Not without a compelling reason."

"So there is something?" With Sheila unresponsive, Dave ran the math. Jennifer had been gone from the Aldrich for two years. The project Sheila knew about might have pre-dated that. Jenn might have been there for the early stages.

"If I tell you why I want to know, will you tell me?"

"Depends."

"What happens in this office stays in this office?" he said.

"That's fair."

"What if I tell you that my fifteen year old daughter may have HIV?"

She paused. At first, she showed no reaction and then, as if on cue, she expressed concern. "Liv?"

He nodded.

"It makes no sense. Oh, Dave. I'm so sorry."

He looked for judgment on her face. Or even surprise. He saw neither. It was as if she already knew. "Can you help?" he asked.

"Of course."

She did not ask how it happened. He assumed she wanted to know, that she was being polite while preparing to pass judgment on Liv.

"We don't know how it happened," he said.

Jennifer seemed to reset. "How hard can it be? There's only…"

Dave felt a small rage threaten inside of him, felt his face flush. Jennifer backed off. "I'm being insensitive. You need a solution. Not a post-mortem."

"Is there really a cure?" Dave fixed his gaze fixed on her.

"Maybe," she said at last. "Despite Claire's denials, it's one of the major ongoing drug discovery activities at the Aldrich. A friend of mine is the chief scientist on it."

Sheila, he thought. "Can I get to it?"

"I don't know. It's been nearly ready for clinical trials for some time, but Aldrich politics seem to be slowing it down."

"Not the FDA?"

"Not this time. The FDA has been very flexible about moving AIDS drugs into clinicals. The scientist I mentioned isn't even sure why there's any delay. She's ready to go with it."

"Sheila?"

"I can't tell you."

"You already have."

Jennifer's eyes narrowed in thought and she said nothing in response.

"Well, what do I do?" Dave asked. "I need to have her get Liv in the trials when they start."

"She can't help you there. Not yet. If she leaks, she's fired. This is Claire's call. And you can't let her know you know about this. I'm not even supposed to know anything current about it."

"So how do I get Claire to tell me about it? When I asked her about a cure before, she stonewalled me."

"Did you tell her about Liv?"

"I did." Dave saw real surprise and a hint of anger on Jennifer's face.

"When was this?"

"Three weeks ago. On the day of Evan's memorial service."

"Interesting," Jennifer said. She walked to the window and looked toward the mountains. She said nothing for a full 30 seconds.

"You're upset?" he finally asked. "Did you expect Claire to confide in you? I know you two are close, but I specifically asked her not to tell anyone. She honored my confidence."

She turned back to him. "You need to meet with her again."

"Clearly."

Jennifer looked worried. "Please, please, remember that you cannot tell her you know, let alone that I'm the source. I don't want anyone losing their job because I'm trying to help you."

"I promise."

After Jennifer left the office, Dave dialed Claire McQuaid's direct line. Her voice mail answered.

"Claire," he said, "Dave Clement. There's something I need to discuss with you. Urgently. How about coffee tomorrow morning? Call me. Or text."

As he hung up the phone, he wondered what he would do if Claire stonewalled him again. He would have to tell her what he knew. She would deduce that Jennifer was the source, not Sheila. That would protect Sheila. And Jennifer was safe at Prodeus. If Claire got pissed off at Jennifer, he would protect her from any career repercussions. Jennifer would make her fortune with the Prodeus IPO anyway. She would not need Claire McQuaid. After all, he thought, how much damage could Claire really do?

CHAPTER 27

Fort Collins: Clements' home
November 19, 11:40 p.m.

Dave did not sleep well that first night home. After dinner, he had updated Mel on the activity with Jennifer and Sheila. Claire still had not returned his last two calls. It was unusual for her not to get back to him the same day.

After that, he went upstairs to bed while Mel stayed at her desk in the study. He had expected her to join him in bed, hoped to make love. He left the bed twice, making the journey down the stairs to the study to check on her. Impatiently, she told him she had work to finish. He understood. When, on the day after Liv landed in the emergency room, he called to ask Mel if she would let him back in the house, he expected her to bite his head off about his earlier decision to stay away. Instead, she simply said, "Good. Your daughter needs you." He should have recognized the other half of the message she intended for him. Yes, Liv needed him, but Mel did not. Now, lying naked under the covers, he felt more and more awkward as the clock ticked past midnight. He opened his tablet to read a book. A page into it, he nodded off. About one, he woke again, the tablet lying on his chest. He heard movement in Liv's room. Pulling on a pair of boxers, he went down the hall. He found Mel kneeling at Liv's bedside, her head bowed in prayer.

Kneeling beside her, he gently placed his arm around her waist. Her head tilted on to his shoulder. He felt her warm tears on his bare skin as they trickled off his shoulder and over the swell of his chest. Together they remained silently on their knees for a few more minutes. Both contemplated the innocent child that lay sleeping before them, seeming both more fragile and more peaceful than at any waking hour. She slept silently, not even having the very slight snoring Mel had acquired over the last few years, let alone the bear-like growl of her father's snore. Despite her rare outbursts of teenage rebellion, Dave knew she trusted them completely, secure in knowing they were always there for her. His long absences raised doubts about that trust. Tonight he was back – and Mel told him that Liv had fallen asleep more readily than she had in months.

Why haven't you paid more attention? The challenge to himself rose inside Dave. The extra hours at the office, the hurt looks, nights in foreign cities, the missed games and all the other school events. The nights in front of the TV, home from the office at eight, eating dinner before some mindless sitcom – and Liv, tiny and delicate in her elementary school years, tugging on his arm to talk, confiding with her small little girl voice, just to tell him about something or to ask for help with homework.

Not now, he always said. Not now. I'm too tired. Let me watch this show first.

Then he would fall asleep in the chair, the TV still on. When he awoke, the lights were down, Mel in bed, having tucked Liv in while he napped. He would stop in Liv's room and look at her, whisper he loved her, hoping she heard him in her sleep. Those years had just skipped by, stolen by time and his preoccupation.

"I'm sorry," he mumbled aloud involuntarily.

"What?" Mel whispered.

His reverie broken, he looked at Mel, saw her wet eyes glistening in the dark.

"I think I was dreaming," he whispered.

He nodded his head toward the door, stood up and tugged Mel's hand. Then he bent over and lightly touched the side of Liv's foot, protruding from under her blanket like it always did. He wanted so much to talk to her now, to squeeze her close.

Mel followed him through the dark hallway to the master bedroom. They crawled into the same side of the king-size bed, a long gone phenomenon. They kissed softly once. Mel nestled against his chest and they drifted off to sleep.

CHAPTER 28

Prodeus Boardroom, Loveland
November 20, 9:12 a.m. Mountain Time

Dave tapped the "end" icon on his cell phone. He laid the phone on his desk and took in a deep breath. Claire had finally returned his call. He pondered the phone for a moment and then slammed his fist down on the desk.

"Thanks for nothing, Claire," he said. Claire had provided good news on the business side, but the personal side did not go as he had hoped. She still stonewalled him on the AIDS work.

He got up and walked down the hall to the boardroom. As he entered, Dan Dorfmann, chief financial officer of Prodeus, clicked off the overhead projector and the room faded to black. Jennifer got up from the conference table and flipped the light switch. The softer indirect boardroom lights blinked on.

"Nice of you to show up, Dave."

"Cover anything we didn't talk about earlier, Dan." Dave did not feel like taking any more crap from anyone this morning.

"No."

"Then I'm good."

Brian Middleton, Ed Hepp, Dave, and Nick Goodman, the manufacturing VP, all sat quietly as Dave found a seat.

"The more I think about it, the more it bothers me," Ed said. "We need to shop other underwriters."

Dorfmann ran a hand back over his smooth scalp. First, he shook his head 'no' and then he nodded 'yes' as though he were running trial balloons with himself before speaking. "I hate to do it, Ed," he said. "Each underwriter's going to be giving us their own version of a rectal exam - and that's resource intensive."

"You don't always get to go back to the well. We need to maximize our execution price. Thatcher Ripley may be working against us on that."

Brian interrupted, "This is all new to me, guys. What difference does it make? If Thatcher Ripley prices us too low, we'll find our level in the market after the public offering, won't we?"

Dorfmann smirked, "Now I know why you're an engineer, Brian."

Brian grinned politely as the rest of the room laughed, except for Dave. "Did you always know the answer, Dan?" Brian asked, returning Dan's smirk.

"From conception. My father - "

"Let's not go there," Jennifer quickly intercepted the subsequent series of potentially off-color comments. Guffaws followed. Again Dave did not join in.

Dorfmann continued, "Anyway, the company only gets the execution price. What happens after that is between individual shareholders. In this case, Thatcher Ripley would have us leave over $50 million on the table."

"I don't understand," Nick said.

Dorfmann explained. "Our corporate windfall is the opening or execution price times the number of shares we offer. Thatcher Ripley is coming up $7 per share short of where we think we should be. With 8 million shares being offered to the public. 8 million times the $7 shortfall is over $50 million. Money out of our pocket that they're trying to steer toward their own favored clients. Even if the stock goes up $100 per share in the hour after opening, the company gets none of it."

"What about the employees?" Nick Goodman asked.

"Employees get the stock for whatever it's worth when we individually sell it. But insider trading rules lock employees out for six months after the IPO. We cannot sell share one until the stock's been in the market for two quarters. It's prudent so that we don't look like we're profiting individually before the stock has a public track record."

"I'm still confused," Brian said. "I'm still not sure what the problem with Thatcher Ripley is. I thought we didn't price until the day before we went public."

"You're right," Dorfmann said. "But underwriters always give you a ballpark as to what they think you're worth. Plus they fundamentally pre-sell to key large investors which essentially fixes the price assumptions well in advance of the offering itself. Those investors are guaranteed the stock at the opening price no matter what happens in the hours that follow. If Thatcher Ripley underprices it to take care of their large investors, the price could soar day one and we get none of it, while the large investors who got the starting price are in a position for rich profit-taking. Bottom-line: We think Thatcher Ripley is short-changing us to the tune of about $56 million to take care of their large investors."

Dave joined the conversation. "There's another motivation I can think of," he said. "They have a major interest in the Aldrich, our principal partner and most likely acquirer, whether we're publicly held or private. By keeping the price down, maybe they think they can cause us to sell out to the Aldrich instead of going public. Problem is we would not get nearly as much individually for our shares. Plus a lot of folks would lose their jobs in the new company."

"Wait a minute," Jennifer said. "The Aldrich doesn't play those games."

"I didn't say the Aldrich, Jennifer. I'm talking about Thatcher Ripley. It's investment banking. They play hardball. It would almost be surprising if they didn't try to keep the price down."

"That's illegal!" Brian declared.

Ed spoke, his tone flat, "No, Brian, it's not. The burden's on us to look out for our own interests."

Ed sat back, slowly twiddling his oversized thumbs on his Buddha belly. His hands trembled slightly. He looked to Dorfmann to move the meeting along on a different track.

"Conspiracy theories aside," Dorfmann said, "we owe it to ourselves to shop this deal some more. If Nick can move the manufacturing ramp up a week and we do get a PR pop at Christmas, it would help valuation. And make the Aldrich more dependent on us."

"More dependent might be a little strong," Jennifer suggested. "But the press coverage will help both companies."

Ed turned to Dave. "We talked about Claire's request to move manufacturing up by a week before you came in. Nick says it can be done. Not easy, but do-able. We think we can get holiday PR for the humanitarian side of our story. That could help us attract alternative underwriters for the IPO, or strengthen our hand with Thatcher Ripley. Plus keep Claire and the Aldrich happy."

"Perfect," Dave said. "Thanks, Ed." Dave forced a smile. Other things weighed on him and the rest of this all seemed secondary this morning.

As everyone filed out of the boardroom, Dave called to Jennifer out in the hall. "Give me a minute over here."

He pulled her back into the empty boardroom. They spoke in hushed tones.

"Claire and I talked this morning."

"I wondered when that would happen," she said. "How'd it go?"

"She gave me nothing. Said you probably drew some incorrect assumptions from the roadmaps they were showing when you were still there."

Jennifer stepped back, her hand on her heart and her mouth wide open in horror. "You told her that I said the Aldrich was working on an AIDS cure? I told you that in strictest confidence. What the hell?"

Dave's face reddened. He had not told Claire outright, but he certainly let her box him in a little.

"No. No, I didn't. I never admitted you were the source. She just assumed it."

She turned away, waving her fists in the air. "Oh, Dave," she said, still speaking in quiet tones. "You've really screwed me. You've screwed all of us. She'll never trust me again."

"Look, she doesn't know for sure that you said anything. I didn't even tell her that anyone said anything. I referenced old press releases that said the Aldrich was working on a cure."

"Then how did I come up?"

"At one point, she just assumed it was you." And, he thought, not Sheila. A good outcome.

"I'm so screwed."

He placed his hand on her shoulder. "Look, I don't think you are, but if you are, we'll deal with it. Your future's here anyway. You'll make so much money with the IPO that you won't care about Claire."

She looked down at his hand. He quickly withdrew it.

"You offering a consolation prize," she asked, stepping closer to him.

Dave looked at her face and smelled her perfume. He looked into her green eyes and felt himself drawn to her.

She reached around and hugged him.

He felt guilty as hell for what he had done to her; McQuaid probably would push her out of the circle.

"Oh, man," he said, pulling away with a sigh. "No. No consolation prize. If you think I'm a jerk, leave it at that. I'm not going to make up for it like this."

As he backed toward the door, Jennifer tried another tactic. "You're a coward, aren't you? You want to be with me, but you're afraid."

He stopped long enough to measure his response. "You're right," he said. "I am afraid. I'm afraid of doing something stupid and messing up the best thing that ever happened to me."

She moved closer, the scent of her perfume growing more intense. "We're not going to hurt the damn company. I'll be discrete."

Dave stepped into the doorway. "You just don't get it," he whispered, looking over his shoulder to make sure no one was around.

"What don't I get?"

"I'm not talking about the company." He turned and headed for the stairs.

After Dave left, Jennifer turned back into the boardroom, tears bubbling up. She chided herself for getting emotional, tried to understand why. Part of it was because she did not want to be alone anymore, because she wanted to be with Dave. Or someone like him. Then she knew why she was crying. She had never seen a man so much in love and so committed to his wife. She cried because she suddenly hated herself for trying to break up his home, trying to destroy something rare and good.

And she cried because she had failed, an uncommon experience for her, especially when dealing with men. She realized that she had no alternative but to move to plan B.

Claire would be disappointed in her.

CHAPTER 29

Fort Collins, Jennifer's Apartment
November 20, 7:48 p.m. Mountain Time

That evening in her apartment, Jennifer downed her third glass of wine and opened her e-mail. She clicked on "new" and typed in Sheila Stratemeier's address in the "To" box.

"Sheila, been a couple weeks since we got together. How about Silver Grill Cafe for breakfast Saturday morning? Try 8:30 to give you time to get down from the pass. Lots to tell. Your instincts proved right one more time. My efforts to lure Dave with my charms have flopped miserably. The loyal b… has, in fact, returned to his wife. I am so not happy with myself.

"We can talk some more about your paranoid fantasies, too. I'm getting pressure from Claire for next drastic step. So I think I understand what you're going through. Maybe I can offer you fresh perspective. But blowing the whistle can only undermine the good we intend. Don't do it. Love, Jenn."

She clicked "send."

CHAPTER 30

Rome: A café just outside Vatican City
November 21, 7:45 a.m. Central European Time

"Grazie mille," the man said as Father Jim pressed a two euro tip into his hand.

"Prego," Jim responded, the 'r' trilled by his native Irish accent.

The priest walked out to the old Roman street. No smog today. The morning's rain had washed it away. He thought that the sky's color must have been the same blue that inspired the blue in Michelangelo's work in the Sistine Chapel. Crossing the narrow street, he walked toward the main entrance to Vatican City. At this hour, the towering exterior walls of the Vatican provided shade across the entire street, a tremendous gift in the heat of summer, but a bit chilly now.

The buildings along his way stood three to five stories high, mostly apartments with small shops on the bottom floor. Some of them seemed integrated with the Vatican walls, probably papal property. Subtle shades of yellow, orange and red spun swirling frescoes on the stucco, outlining the ancient brown brick that occasionally peeked from beneath centuries of exterior repairs and changes.

The smells wafting from the tiny restaurants still appealed to him, even after a late afternoon dinner of spaghetti Bolognese, the consistency of its pasta and the spices in its thin red sauce done exactly to Jim's taste as only the Romans could do. In the early mornings when Jim went out for his walks, the rich, sweet aroma of bread and pastries still in the oven filled the air. Now, the bouquet of tomato sauce cooking permeated the streets and alleys as the restaurants prepared for the evening.

Most of the restaurants had some outdoor dining with tables adorned in red and white check or simply red, the inevitable candle stuck in an empty Chianti bottle that acted as a centerpiece. Small glaciers of white wax coated the bottom of the candles and the round sides of the bottles. New candles would destroy the ambiance. Jim wondered if it was someone's job to burn the candles down before putting them on the tables. Pausing to look at a menu posted on the sidewalk, Jim spoke with an attractive dark-haired hostess, her ample and visible pink cleavage adorned with a green jeweled cross on a gold chain. He asked about the house sauce and the Saltimbocca. She reached behind him for the menu, brushing against him, reminding him of how much the vow of chastity limited him.

He glanced at the menu, asked a few more culinary questions and backed away, nearly bowling over a young woman taking pictures.

"Disculpe, Signorina," he said, excusing himself.

"It's my own fault," the anorexic-looking woman in black said. "I was too busy followin' in the lens instead o' watchin' where I was goin'.'"

Jim recognized the accent immediately. "You're Irish!" he said.

"Sure."

"It's nice to hear a voice from the old sod."

She touched his arm, her fingertips gentle. "Where ya from, Father?"

Jim hesitated. Finally well-rested, his male hormones seemed to have come to life. He liked her touch on his arm. Skinny, but very pretty, a fire in her dark eyes. Feeling a slight shiver, he shook off her hand.

"Oh, someplace you never heard of," he said, pangs of guilt and desire tugging at him. "I need to hurry along. Enjoy your visit."

As he stumbled out of hearing range, she mumbled, "Ya rude bastard"

Turning left away from the Vatican, Jim walked down a side street toward Castel San Angelo and the Tiber River.

"Father, give me strength," he mumbled, picking up his pace to churn off sexual energy.

The round, crenelated castle, built as a mausoleum for the Roman Emperor Hadrian in the second century, had been used for a millennium as a fortress for the Popes. Cesare Borgia, the illegitimate son of Pope Alexander the VI had used it to torture prisoners, mostly political enemies. Borgia, the inspiration for Machiavelli's The Prince, had been cutting off hands and cutting out tongues long before the current fashion in sub-Saharan Africa.

Jim constantly worried about the Karanjas. Vatican intelligence, not always accurate or current as with any intelligence organization, had learned the rebels had coveted Lokoma for some reason. He wondered if the government troops had been able to push the rebels back before they reached the village. He doubted they even showed up. If they had failed, then Hamara, stubborn as he was, probably had stayed and been killed. Jim prayed that he had been wise enough to get his family out.

He reached into his pocket and pulled out a small clear baggie. He bounced it in his hand. When he was dressing to leave the hospital, the nurse handed him the contents from his pockets, emptied before his clothes were sent away for cleaning: a handful of Leonean change, breath mints, and the little plastic baggie of pills he had been bringing to little Sara. He knew that without the quinine sulfate, Sara's odds of survival were not good.

Arriving at the Pont Sant Angelo, an ancient bridge across the Tiber, Jim leaned on the stone railing. He pondered the polluted water flowing slowly beneath. He had sent appeals directly to the Pope, but the only response he received supported his superior's decision. He would not return to Sierra Leone. The rebels had specifically targeted him. Anyone associating with him would be in danger. The Vatican could not "responsibly allow him to take that risk."

He wondered how they could "responsibly" not. The bureaucrats of the

Church failed in that regard. They did not understand evangelism at the ground level. Without Jim's presence, Karanja's tribe would attribute everything to evil spirits or juju. They would drift away from Christ again, blaming the priest and Jesus both for making the spirits angry. Hamara's authority would be undermined and anarchy would ensue. Even if that did not happen, Jim knew that the souls of Jacob and Ani would be at risk as they struggled to understand why Hamara's conversion had broken up the family in such an ultimately useless gesture.

In the late afternoon sun, he gazed at a fuzzy reflection of himself in the water far below. He watched as a woman came alongside him. Too close, he thought as he looked up. It was the same woman he had bumped into earlier.

"Are you followin' me?" he asked, a bit flattered by the girl's persistence.

"That I am," she said, sparkling coal black eyes honing in.

He sized her up. Not more than about five-foot two and not a pound over ninety-five. Probably a college student.

"I suppose you're not likely to be muggin' me since I'm quite a bit larger than you."

She smiled and stepped back, looking at him through her camera lens now. "In a way, I am," she said. "I'm takin' a picture o' your mug, anyway."

Jim smiled back. Her engaging manner appealed to him. It would be nice to talk with someone who did not carry a Vatican employee pass.

A middle aged couple walked by. The young woman ran up to them with her camera. "Per favore, per favore," she said, motioning aggressively.

The man quickly understood and took the camera. The young woman ran up beside Fr. Jim and latched on to his arm, smiling broadly while kicking one foot in the air, its shoe left behind on the pavement. The man snapped the picture and the girl waved her index finger in the air.

"Due, per favore," she said.

Placing her lips on the flustered priest's cheek, she held the pose until the shutter clicked again. The woman looked askance at the girl and the priest, clucking at her husband in Italian as they walked away.

"I hope that you don't plan to give those to my superior," Jim said in jest, but still slightly dismayed.

"Just souvenirs, Father."

Suddenly, she turned and thrust out her hand. "My name is Colleen," she declared as he accepted her grip. "I'm a tourist."

"Jim Reilly, priest," he said.

"Can I buy you an espresso, Father?" she asked, tucking her camera in her bag.

"I really shouldn't," he said.

"I'm not here to threaten your vow of chastity," she said. "I don't speak Italian very well. It would be nice to speak English with someone who knows their way around."

"How do you know I'm not just a visitor, too?"

She laughed and leaned back on the stone rail, looking up at him, the orange glow of the setting sun reflecting off her eyes and her glowing, youthful cheeks.

"Your Vatican badge is a dead giveaway," she said, nodding toward the badge that hung from his belt. He had forgotten to take it off.

"Caught," he said.

"Now about that espresso?"

"There's a little cafe just on the other side of the bridge."

"No tourists?"

"No sightings recently," he answered.

"Perfect."

On the short walk to the café, she probed him about life in the Vatican. Did he ever see the Pope close-up? Had he ever concelebrated Mass with the Pope? How many other Irish were in the Vatican? Did women have any influence on decisions? What kind of roles did they have?

At the café, they ordered their drinks and she slipped off to the restroom. As she returned, she stopped to talk to a rugged looking man sitting at the bar.

"What was that?" he asked as she sat down.

"Tried to pick me up in Italian. I used one of the few phrases I know. Stopped him cold."

They laughed. As they sat at the short, narrow table sipping espressos, she asked, "How about you? What do you do for the Vatican?"

"Try to save souls in dangerous places. It's a sort of penance."

"Do they send you or do you choose to go, Father?"

He played with his saucer. "Very insightful, Colleen," he said. "In a sense, I suppose I choose for myself."

"What are ya doin' penance for?" she asked, her face suddenly very serious.

He studied her for a moment and then looked down. Would there ever be enough confession for what he had done? He felt forgiven by God, but he still had a price to pay. Maybe that explained the origins of the concept of purgatory. People did not conceive it as a place that allowed them to stay out of hell. They conceived it as a place to continue to work out the unresolved guilt from this life while still in a state of grace. Maybe God could forgive them, but imperfect people could not always forgive themselves.

He looked back at her, her face stern with anticipation. "It's a long time ago," he said. "A very long time."

"Sometimes it seems like just a minute ago, doesn't it," she said, shaking her head affirmatively.

Jim picked up his coffee cup. "You're right about that. As young as ya are, ya must have a share of your own pain to know."

"I do. And I expect it to get worse before it gets better. Sometimes moral surgery is quite painful, but we still have to do it, don't we? Do ya think your brother Mike feels it, too?"

Jim's grip on the coffee cup tightened. He put it down. "How d'ya know I have a brother, let alone his name?"

She picked up her camera bag and purse as she rose from her seat. "Your secrets are catchin' up to ya, Sean."

"What's this about?" he asked. "Where did you hear that name?" He stood and grabbed her by the forearm.

"It's okay," she said, "You should let go before one of the fellas in here feels a need to defend a helpless woman."

"I've done nothing to you. They can see that."

"No, Father," she said, shaking her arm loose. "They see what I want them to see."

She kicked the table over in front of him and ran out the front door, dodging down a narrow alley. Jim tripped over the table but recovered quickly. As he approached the door, the rugged guy who had tried to pick the girl up blocked his path.

"She told me you might be up to no good, Father," he said in Italian. "Let her be. She doesn't want anything to do with a priest. Think of your vows."

"How could she tell you that? She doesn't speak Italian."

The man laughed. "Maybe not to you, but she spoke it like a native to me."

Fr. Jim pushed the man out of the way. By the time he did, the woman had disappeared.

CHAPTER 31

Rawah Wilderness of northern Colorado: Cameron Pass
November 22, 11:10 p.m. Mountain Time

In the thin air of Cameron Pass, where the peaks of the Colorado Rockies first scrape Wyoming sky, Sheila struggled late into the night with information she did not fully understand. Information about death. A lot of death. Avoidable death.

Her lab coat thrown over her cubicle wall, Sheila propelled her thin fingers in a manic jig across the keyboard. The phosphorescent blue light of the PC's display revealed squinting eyes and lips squeezed together over grinding teeth. The ethereal glimmer stood a beacon among a sea of cubicles in Dilbertville, a ghost town until morning shift arrived in just a few hours. The gloomy expanse echoed with the creaking of expanding and contracting metal vents, the vague howl of the mountain wind in counterpoint – each new variation causing Sheila to flash her eyes for a nervous glance along the battlements of her cubicle fortress.

She had nearly escaped. At 6:30, she started to leave the building for the lab's dorms, but the chill of autumn wind rushing across the compound gave her pause at the exit. The wrestling match in her conscience drove her back inside.

Having come to know many AIDS victims in the course of her research, Sheila knew the horrible, wasting death that inevitably resulted. Any hope mattered.

But not this.

The Aldrich plan jumped the gun. It could easily kill tens of thousands, maybe hundreds of thousands, in Sierra Leone and its near neighbors in West Africa. In one model that Sheila ran, the number of dead exceeded one million. Exactly the opposite of what she worked so hard to accomplish.

But Eldridge and Claire remained unbending in their determination to deploy Vif-D prematurely, damn the consequences. The science was complicated and inherently risky. Deliberately skipping steps made the risk unacceptable to Sheila. She remained unwilling to eradicate people in order to eradicate disease

Her team had successfully created a protein mutation inside the HIV cells that would make all those with Group M HIV, the largest HIV group in sub-Saharan Africa, vulnerable to the Aldrich vaccine strategy.

The catch was that the protein mutation, Vif-D, had to first universally replace natural Vif in the HIV cells, and then exist alone in the victim long enough to cause the body to stabilize its response to the mutation. This would result in the body creating the antibodies necessary for Sheila to finalize the synthesis of CEM15-D, the protein that when accompanied by the Vif-D protein, wiped out HIV. But without proper preparation using the antibodies, the body would reject CEM15-D, leaving Vif-D alone to ravage its victims.

That meant the blood of the new victims had to be drawn as soon as the body's response stabilized, and the CEM15-D synthesis needed to be completed quickly in the lab before the Vif-D version of HIV could do measurable damage. Each individual's antibodies were not needed, but a broad sampling across a population segment was needed to ensure effectiveness.

Unfortunately, while Sheila's team had initially deployed CEM15-D successfully in a small secret trial with a remote tribe in Panama, something had gone wrong subsequently. Five members of the Kuna tribe died as a result, years too soon. Sheila had yet to figure out how to again get the bio-engineered gene to reliably adhere to human T-cells. Her team had isolated the problem to issues in the RNA transcription process used, but it would still take months to solve them. And without CEM15-D, the Vif-D mutation introduced in the Trojan horse would have free reign to kill at a very rapid and high rate.

Yet, while she remained confident the adherence problem would eventually be solved, Claire and Eldridge now were steering an ethically deplorable course. She did not understand the rush at all. The genocidal risk the Aldrich seemed willing to take with the lives of over a million people, starting with the Lokoma tribe in Sierra Leone, violated every principal of drug discovery or any kind of medicine.

Sheila hardly slept any more, desperately working on the CEM15-D fix, but she had serious doubts that the fix could happen quickly enough. Sheila had met with Claire repeatedly, but Claire remained determined to deploy the Vif-D protein inside the new malaria vaccine without a guarantee on the timing of the CEM15-D gene. She planned to follow through with the original timetable to use the new vaccine as a Trojan horse to introduce the deadly new HIV.

So Sheila did not know where to turn, especially after Evan Conger's death. She remained convinced that Conger's plane had been sabotaged, that Claire played for keeps. If she were willing to kill a million, one more life to clear a path would be an easy decision for her. Sheila took some small comfort in the knowledge that Claire needed her alive and functioning to finish CEM15-D.

She had hoped that she could recruit Dave Clement to help her, but then uncovered the issues with his daughter. For weeks now, she had tried to figure out how to warn him and tell him what he needed to know. But any open communications could endanger both of them. In desperation, she had placed a new folder on the cloud earlier that night, but neither Dave nor anyone else would be able to access it without knowing one of her secrets.

So Sheila decided to try Pamela Thatcher who sat on the Aldrich board.

Some claimed that she both elected and controlled US Presidents. Certainly, both political and economic power resided in her grasp. For Sheila, Pamela stood out among women as a leader and human being.

Sheila wanted to assume that Pamela did not know about any of this, that she would stop it in its tracks if she knew. Sheila suspected that Claire probably sanitized the board presentations to keep Pamela in the dark. Short of going to the press, which would be bad for everyone including Sheila, getting Pamela to intervene was Sheila's last best hope.

So, for once, she did not spend the evening working on the CEM15-D fix. Instead, she spent it writing an extensive document detailing the risks of the plan in its current state and the challenge of getting CEM15-D deployed in time, both in terms of testing and actual distribution.

Now, it was nearly midnight. Sheila adjusted the desk lamp so that its narrow band of dim light landed where she needed it on the reference papers beside her computer monitor.

Several hours earlier, she had called her brother, a Catholic pastor in Pittsburgh. She could trust him to keep her confidence and she needed an advisor. He was a priest, a confessor. The information would be treated like the confidences of a confessional. There was no risk to the Aldrich. Her brother listened to her for nearly forty-five minutes and encouraged her to do what she thought was right. She practiced her arguments on him, finally getting entirely comfortable with the case she would present. He clearly agreed that the issue was a moral and ethical one. He suggested she might be both stressed out and, consequently, paranoid in her fears about the Aldrich's intent. No responsible enterprise would do the things she feared, he told her. There must be more to the plan.

She took little solace in his perspective, choosing to go ahead with the document. If her brother's optimism about the Aldrich proved right, she would be tagged as a conspiracy theorist, a nut. She could live with that.

She finished writing a summary of the document. A long sigh. She dropped back in her chair, hands flung to her lap. After a moment, she raised her hands, held them poised over the keyboard to finalize the email with an introduction.

A thud. She looked up. Waited. Quiet.

Her fingers dropped to the keyboard, pouring a flow of words across the screen.

Claire, Pamela and the rest of the Aldrich Institute board would have this when they arrived at their offices in the morning. If they failed to respond, she would have no choice but to go to the press and expose the whole plan, one in which she had played an instrumental role. She already had gone so far as to load the phone numbers of the Denver Post and the mile-high city's Fox TV affiliate on her cell.

She did not really want to involve the press. She did not want the headlines for herself or the lab. They would undermine the great good the lab could do. Plus, she would end up blackballed for life and probably cause Claire and the Aldrich to fight her all the harder. Working through internal channels — that felt right. No outsiders. No headlines.

The dance of her fingers accelerated on the keys, the flow of words streaming across the screen.

The plastic bridge of her glasses slipped down her nose. A finger popped off the keyboard to push them back up.

A quiet thud. Nearby. She paused, scanned the top of her cubicle walls. Quiet.

Fingers poised again. Face back in the blue light.

A knock. She half rose from her seat, hovering, listening. A loud clatter. She stood, grabbed the top of the cubicle and peered over.

Her shoulders relaxed. She tapped on the top of the cube. Waved. Several cubicles away, a man wearing a gray institutional shirt waved back. He dumped a plastic trash can into a larger container. Sheila blew out, sat, fingers back on the keyboard.

The incessant rhythm of the clicking keys slowed only slightly when she sensed the movement behind her. She felt no pain when the wire sliced through her windpipe. When her body jerked from its chair, the garrote caught in the parts of her neck. Her hand reached out to hit the send key, barely missing. Airborne, she vaguely registered her loafers dangling off the toes of her naked feet. Her toes curled, trying to save the shoes. New shoes. An instant later, her air-starved nerves imploded, one final burst of confused data firing across screaming synapses.

In the end, Sheila made headlines after all.

CHAPTER 32

Shadyside, Pennsylvania: Rectory of Sacred Heart Catholic Church
November 22, 9:55 p.m. Eastern Time

Almost 1,500 miles away in the Shadyside neighborhood of Pittsburgh, Fr. Bill Stratemeier, dressed in black slacks and shirt with white roman collar, stepped out the front door of his rectory to light his pipe. He was a new pastor and his assistant had asked him not to smoke in the house. He could have ignored the younger man, but he preached that the higher one's rank the greater one's duty to serve the interests of others.

Anyway, he thought, it's a nice night.

Strolling through the parish garden, he circled the aging church and inhaled the sweet, mild smoke through the well-chewed plastic stem. With one hand in his pocket, he looked up to see the stars. They were remarkably visible this night in spite of the city lights. A cold front had swept in from the Midwest that afternoon, blowing out the smog and clouds. The few remaining leaves of a buckeye tree rustled over him as he approached the sanctuary of the church.

Through the bright, multi-colored hues of the stained glass, he could see the reassuring flickering of candlelight. Tonight he needed the peace. He feared he may have betrayed his sister's confidence, but the situation seemed far more serious than he let on when he talked to her earlier that evening. Sheila had always been very trusting and, while she seemed to know something was wrong at her secret research facility, she could not possibly comprehend the full scope of the issue. If Sheila was suspicious, then something really bad must be afoot.

Father Bill had heard rumors of plots to spare the world millions of lives lost in wars through carefully targeted genocide by medicine. Just eliminate the world's problem people and there would be nothing left to fight over. Commerce and the practical aspects of the marketplace would then be able to effectively rule.

Fast-acting AIDS hidden in a malaria vaccine sounded suspiciously like the kind of vehicle that would fit the scenario.

Within the secret councils of the Holy Mother Church, intelligence was gathered and shared. Only recently had Bill become involved. Bill had been an increasingly active participant in the pro-life movement until a year earlier when his bishop again gently tried to get him to abandon the extreme fringes of the movement.

"You don't stand on a soapbox against violence to babies while consorting with those who would advocate violence against baby killers," the bishop advised. "Killing is killing, and it's wrong."

So Bill had asked him how else he could fight the killing.

The bishop had answered predictably, "We have to fight it with strong pronouncements from the pulpit, hoping to steer the collective consciousness to enlightenment..."

But then he continued, surprising Father Bill, "...There is another way to put your passion to good use, however..."

And he introduced him to the highly secretive Christus organization. Christus' invitation-only membership included lay people and priests, men and women, in an effort to fight far more nefarious forces at work on the globe. The forces Christus opposed would, if they could, impose the death penalty on people simply for being poor, uneducated, or simply in the wrong geography. The foes of Christus maintained a world vision of a so-called meritocracy built around the accumulation of wealth and the arrogance of technology. God had no place in their world.

Disbelieving, Bill attended a small meeting of five people at the Chancery to satisfy his curiosity. He left that meeting not nearly as skeptical. A network of Catholics, many involved in businesses or other ventures with those of the world vision, continued to collect intelligence and funnel it into central information centers in each diocese. This information was then consolidated in Rome and disseminated very quietly to the members of Christus.

But drug-induced genocide, just one of the dangers uncovered, had only been talk until now. Could his sister have stumbled across the real thing?

Father Bill blessed himself, praying for his sister's well-being. Her board members would see her email. He thought they would respond quickly and constructively. If they did not, then Sheila's worst fears would have some validation. She promised to call him as soon as she heard anything.

Violating his sister's confidence, Bill had advised Christus immediately. His contact thanked him and encouraged him, volunteering prayers for Sheila. At Bill's urging, he agreed to await word of the board members' reaction before passing the issue on to Rome for review.

Bill put his pipe back to his lips and started back down the dark path to the rectory. He felt his back scrape something as he did so. He tried to turn to see what it was, but found he could not move. Suddenly, he felt the air rush from his lungs and the pain in his back grew sharp. He wanted to vomit. Then he did, but it was blood pouring from his lungs. For an instant, he comprehended his situation.

"Oh, dear Jesus," he gasped before he fell dead at the feet of his assailant.

CHAPTER 33

Fort Collins, Silver Grill Café
November 24, 8:31 Mountain Time

At twenty minutes, the wait time at the Silver Grill Café seemed tolerable to Jennifer, dressed comfortably in a brown leather jacket, loose fitting jeans and a flannel shirt as red as her hair. Even her shoes were "granola" this morning, wearing a pair of ankle high hiking boots.

Huddled in front of the register with others waiting for a table, Jennifer drank free coffee. She looked at the time: 8:33. Sheila had a long drive and there had been snow in the mountains overnight. Under those conditions, Jennifer did not expect her to be punctual..

Finally seated at 8:45, Jennifer ordered fresh squeezed orange juice and more coffee. She tapped the screen on her phone. Finding her tasks app, she checked off completed tasks or those no longer necessary. For others, she moved the due date further into the future. For the task "**Prepare Liv Clement for clinical trial,**" she re-set it for early December follow-up. The focus today needed to be on salvaging Sheila before the woman dug too deep a hole for herself. The program's second step rode squarely on Sheila's shoulders as did one of the final outcomes of Jennifer's plan B. She needed Sheila to help her avoid turning into a killer.

Unconsciously sipping her coffee, she finished reviewing her tasks in ten minutes. 8:55. The two women had met here once in the days between the plane crash and Evan's memorial service. At that meeting, Sheila had re-expressed her concern about the practices in the lab.

"There's something very wrong," she had said.

"You can't just give me generalizations without details," countered Jennifer.

"You don't want to know the details. It wouldn't be good for you. Trust me."

Jennifer noticed that Sheila's skin had turned completely pale, almost transparent, from constantly being inside the lab. The few hours sunbathing on the Poudre with Jennifer weeks earlier may have been her only break.

"So have you been doing any cross-country skiing?" she asked.

"Heck no. My exercise amounts to early morning walks at 9,000 feet. Weather permitting. I've tried to run. At that altitude, it just wears me out for the entire day. And I don't go very far."

"Altitude's tough," Jennifer agreed. "So are you going to tell me?"

Sheila tilted her head and looked at her friend in amazement. "What's the old saying?" she finally said. "I can tell you, but if I do

I'm going to have to shoot you."

"With my love life, that's probably all right. How's the tattoo?"

"Haha. Don't even talk to me about love life. Boy scientists seem to get uglier under prolonged exposure to artificial light."

"So neither of us has a significant other. What do we have to lose? Just tell me what's going on?"

"We've just lost Dr. Conger. That's tough enough."

"I don't get the connection."

Sheila's eyes flashed. "There's a connection."

"What are you saying?"

"Too much. That's what I'm saying."

Sheila stuffed a nearly whole piece of cinnamon toast in her mouth. She held her hands up as if to say, "See, I can't talk at all now."

"You will tell me," Jennifer insisted.

Sheila made noises and pointed to her full mouth, cheeks puffed out.

"You've been in the mountains way too long," Jennifer said. "You're turning into a chipmunk."

Sheila laughed and spit what remained of the toast into a napkin. Jennifer smiled and quietly gazed at her friend.

Sheila shrugged and leaned forward. "Listen," she whispered. "I'll tell you, but promise me you won't try to fix it yourself. If you do, they'll kill you."

"You run the same risk."

"No. No, I don't. They need me. If something happened to me, phase 2 of the vaccine would be delayed for months. That's best case. And with you at Prodeus, there's no one at the lab with the skillset to get it back on track."

"I'm rusty as hell," Jennifer said.

"Not really. You stay involved with the software code. And you're the only one at Prodeus who sees the source code. You know how we're fooling the PDNAs. And you know how I think. We trained and worked side by side planning this; we get the science the same way."

"No one at Prodeus knows I see the source."

"I hope not. That would open Pandora's box. If their lawyers knew you had access to the source code, they'd insist Middleton and his crew have it, too. We'd never keep the lid on this."

Jennifer poured a splash of milk in her coffee. She stirred it before responding. She reached out and took Sheila's hand.

"Honey, isn't that exactly what you're threatening to do? Open Pandora's box by escalating your concerns about the process."

"No, I'm hoping that Claire or the board or both will see it my way. I think Eldridge is the problem in this thing. He is so determined to launch the first phase vaccine on schedule; he doesn't care that it could kill thousands before phase 2 is ready for delivery."

"Thousands?"

Sheila leaned forward and whispered. "Maybe hundreds of thousands. Maybe a million."

"You've been at altitude too long."

"I'm serious."

Jennifer nodded. She squeezed Sheila's hand tighter. "Eldridge needs to get the malaria vaccine to West Africa on time. If he doesn't, we lose the window of opportunity."

"Then we should deliver the malaria vaccine without the Trojan horse."

"You know that won't work."

Sheila pulled her hand away. She thought a moment. She sighed. "No, you're right. It won't."

"Trade-offs, Sheila. A few thousand lives in exchange for tens of millions saved in the future."

"But what if it's more? A lot more. We're playing God."

"For future generations of sub-Saharan Africans, we are God."

That was two weeks earlier. Sheila left, promising not to do anything risky unless she talked to Jennifer first. Jennifer thought the discussion kept Sheila inside the circle. Then, Sheila encrypted an e-mail attachment telling her she believed more than ever that the mortality risk could not be justified under any circumstances. She wrote that she had tried with Claire, but that Claire was fully on board with early deployment of the vaccine with the Trojan horse.

Today, Jennifer needed to make Sheila understand that full support of the program amounted to the only way to save people and minimize the front end death toll. She hoped to persuade her that fighting the inevitable only amounted to certain death for the people about whom Sheila expressed so much concern.

Now, at 9:05, Jennifer worried that her friend might have had an accident in the snow. Her stomach growling, Jennifer waved the waitress over and ordered cinnamon roll toast, chunks of re-cycled cinnamon rolls cut up and toasted. Jennifer liked them best slathered in butter, a guaranteed cholesterol high.

"Anything else?" the waitress asked.

Jennifer looked at her phone again. 9:08. Stress made her hungry. She opened the menu.

FIESTA HASH BROWNS – Hash browns grilled with diced bacon, tomato, bell pepper, onion, cheddar and Jack cheese. Served with toast

More cholesterol. Comfort food. Sounded really good on an empty stomach. Definitely not the paleo diet. She ordered it. As the waitress walked away, Jennifer opened the app for the Coloradoan, the local newspaper. She browsed the headlines. Some group warning about the danger of marijuana tourism. Same old. Nothing major this morning. She double tapped her home button and tapped the phone icon. She scrolled to Sheila's name and tapped again. The phone went straight to voice mail.

Jennifer checked her own voicemail. No new messages.

As the waitress poured her fourth cup of coffee, Jennifer reached for the artificial sweetener and the cream, just for variety after three cups of black. When the hash browns arrived, she wished she had not spoiled the coffee with additives because that much good grease warranted strong black coffee to melt it down. She alternated between forkfuls of hash browns and bites of cinnamon roll dipped lightly in coffee. She glanced up to see if anyone noticed and then decided she did not care if they did. In eight or nine months, she would begin cashing Prodeus stock and she could travel to places where better looking, more intelligent men prevailed. She told herself that the test of intelligence would, of course, be the amount of attention they paid to Jennifer.

9:35. Jennifer pushed her empty plate aside and opened the Coloradoan app again. She scanned a story about encroachment on the habitat of grassland hawks and then tapped a link for Colorado news outside of Fort Collins. She looked at the very first story summary:

Unidentified woman found dead in Walden motel. Foul play is considered likely. The motel manager said the woman arrived during the night checking in with someone else. Police are asking for help with identifying the body described as...

Jennifer's breath caught. The general description fit Sheila. Walden was only about 15 minutes west of the lab. Inhaling, she reminded herself that the description was so general that it also fit several other women she knew.

She called Sheila's mobile again and then her room at the lab. No answer. She tried her desk. Nothing. She tried Mike Farley at the lab to see if security could help, but got his voicemail. She decided not to leave him a message. If Sheila had fatally crossed the powers that be, Farley would not be her friend.

Apprehension overtaking her, Jennifer paid the tab and walked out to her car. A few minutes later, she pulled into the gas station at the corner of routes 14 and 287 at the foot of the Poudre Canyon where the Rockies met the Great Plains. She needed to fill up for the long drive over Cameron Pass to Walden.

CHAPTER 34

Prodeus HQs, Loveland, Colorado
November 24, 10:10 a.m. Mountain Time

When he did his routine check of the cloud repository that morning, Dave felt his heart jump. After more than three long weeks without any contact, Sheila had uploaded a new folder there. The folder named NewMeds was gone, replaced by one inexplicably called "Rout", a misspelling of either route or root. Alone in his office, Dave clicked on it. A pop-up appeared requesting a password.

He dropped back in his chair. "What the hell are you doing, Sheila?"

He drummed his fingers on the edge of his desk. "Okay," he said out loud. "If you uploaded new files and password-protected them, you must have a plan for getting the password to me. You're a brilliant scientist. Your work is all about working with the human genome, the most intricate puzzle ever faced. You've thought this out. You're steps ahead of me. And probably everyone else."

He leaned forward and placed his fingers over the keyboard as though a password would magically pop into his head. He dropped back again, shaking his head at his futility.

"This is good news," he finally said. "You'll get me the password."

He logged out. "Progress," he mumbled. "Progress."

CHAPTER 35

Walden, Colorado
November 24, 11:40 a.m. Mountain Time

One hour and forty-five minutes after leaving the Silver Grill, Jennifer drove on to the main street of Walden, passing deep snow drifts piled along the side of the road and a sign that declared the town the moose viewing capital of the world. Situated on a desolate high mountain basin in an area called North Park, about two-thirds of the way from Fort Collins to Steamboat Springs, Walden had been founded in the 1880s as a ranching and lumber town. Changing little over the years, most of its buildings stood only one story high. Jennifer had stopped here once before on her way to ski at Steamboat, sixty miles to the west.

As she arrived in the center of town, she saw a police car parked outside the restaurant across the street. With the restaurant lot full, she parallel parked in the street on packed snow and walked the short distance to the Moose Creek Café, a "Welcome Hunters" banner and a wagon wheel hanging on its front porch rail. A young policeman sat alone at a table near the front of the otherwise full restaurant. He inhaled forkfuls of pie between sips of coffee. Jennifer turned toward the wall and undid the top three buttons on her flannel shirt. Then she walked over to him.

"Do you mind if I join you?" she said. "The place is full."

Glancing up at her, he paused chewing a mouthful of pie as he nodded affirmation.

"Warm and cozy in here," she said as she sat across from him. "Nice change from the frosty weather outside."

He nodded again, averting his eyes to his pie as Jennifer ordered coffee from a passing waitress. A moment later, the cop, a tall Nordic looking guy in his late twenties, glanced her way again, his eyes briefly hovering where her shirt buttons stopped. He quickly returned his eyes to his plate and drank more coffee.

Oh great, thought Jennifer. A shy one. There was the possibility that he did not like what he saw, but Jennifer knew better. Not everyone was Dave Clement and this guy never even registered her face. "So how's the pie?" she asked.

The officer gulped down another mouthful.

"You look like you might know the town," she said.

"I do," he said, lifting his eyes to her face.

She ran a finger over her bottom lip. "Can I try a bite?"

The cop looked at Jennifer and then at his pie and then back at Jennifer. "Sure," he said, handing her a forkful.

"Mmmm," Jennifer said, "Peach. That's good." She handed the fork back to him. "So what's your name?"

"Donovan. Lieutenant Donovan."

"That your first name or your last?"

"Last," Donovan said. "Sorry. Pete. My first name's Pete."

"Well, I'm Jennifer, Lieutenant Pete Donovan," she said, sticking out a hand. "Nice to meet you. And thanks for the pie."

"You want another bite?"

"No, thanks. Have to watch my figure." She glanced down toward her cleavage and his eyes followed.

"Do you have a lot of officers working for you, Pete?"

"No. Just me and the captain."

"You two must be pretty good to be captain and lieutenant."

"How do you mean?" Pete said. He straightened up in his chair, his shoulders going back as his chest swelled out.

"Well, you could've been private and corporal or something. Town fathers must think a lot of you guys."

Pete grinned. "Y'know, I never thought about that. That's probably right, probably exactly right."

"Of course, this bein' such a quiet town, you probably don't get to do too much real crime work."

Pete pointed a finger at her, a serious look on his face. "You're not from around here are you?"

"Nope."

"Then you don't know what we found early yesterday morning."

"No, I don't."

"A body. A murder victim. Right here."

"Right here?" she asked.

Pete hedged. "Well, not *right* here. It was down the street at the North Park Motel. Maid found her naked on the bed."

"Bad, huh?"

"I've seen worse in traffic accidents. This was more sad than it was anything else. She was raped and her throat was cut with some kind of wire. All torn open, stiff and blue, very blue. Don't think I've ever had one so cold. She felt like concrete. Traffic victims are still warm when I find 'em."

Jennifer felt woozy. "That had to be hard." she said.

"Dead bodies stay in your head. The captain says you never really forget 'em."

"I'll bet you don't."

"You want a drink or something."

"I'll have some of your coffee," she said, lifting his cup to her lips and slowly tilting it back for a sip.

"Why are you in Walden?" he said, swallowing hard. "Going over to Steamboat for skiing?"

"I was. Now, I'm not so sure it's safe around here."

"It's safe enough. Haven't had any other killings here since the 1800s. Just be careful who you make friends with. She probably knew the guy. There weren't any signs of a struggle in the room. He was right up close when he did it."

"Who's the woman?"

"We don't know. Not someone who got out very much, though."

"Why do you say that?"

"Real pale skin. You spend any time in the sun at this altitude and you get some color."

Jennifer's head pulsed as images of Sheila flashed in front of her. Other than the aberrant day when she went sunbathing with Jennifer, Sheila's outdoor activity amounted exclusively to her early morning walks, long before the sun got high enough to do anything for her skin.

Jennifer picked up her cell phone. She looked at the display. No messages or calls from Sheila. She breathed in and out slowly. She needed to stick this out. Just a little longer. She took another sip of his coffee. "Anything about her that would make her easy to ID?" she asked.

Pete looked around the crowded restaurant to be certain no one was listening. A couple at the next table had a constant banter going and paid close attention only to each other. The next closest table had three demanding children under five and an overwhelmed mother.

Pete leaned forward and spoke very quietly. "I can't really say anything. It's supposed to be confidential until the coroner rules."

Jennifer pulled her seat around the table, bumping her knees against the cop's.

"Can't hear very well over there," she said.

She leaned closer, her warm breath on his neck. Pete swallowed hard. She made sure to brush her red hair against his chin as she leaned in. Her breasts barely caressed his right arm. She felt fairly confident that women like her rarely stopped in Walden, at least not alone. And this guy clearly had limited experience with this kind of flirtation.

"Okay," he whispered. "It's weird. Old-timers still use the old phone number exchanges up here. Back in the day, Walden used the old Rocky exchange. So you would dial R-O for 7-6, and remember it that way. For the first three digits of a local phone exchange, people would say 'Rocky 2' instead of '762' like we do today."

"You've completely lost me, Pete."

"The victim," he said. "I'm talking about the victim."

As he explained it, Jennifer suddenly knew exactly what he meant.

"She had an old phone number on her," he said. "Tattooed between her legs. Rocky 28714."

CHAPTER 36

Tidewater Region of Virginia, Thatcher Estate
November 24, 6:45 p.m. Eastern Time

A dusting of snow tinted the grounds of the Thatcher estate a bluish white beneath the early evening moonlight. The soft orange glow of gas coach lamps guided guests along the path of the mile long driveway that led to the columned entryway of Tidewater.

Hardy, century old magnolias that never gave up their leaves fenced the edge of nearly the entire driveway until they gave way to great Ponderosa pines. The pines lined the circle around which the drive revolved at the end of its trail. Under the weight of snow and a light wind, the pine boughs bounced, casting dancing shadows in the flickering gaslight around the circle.

At the front of the home, an enormous crystal chandelier glimmered through a vast arched window two-and-one-half stories high. These towered above the grand hall where the loud bumble of visitors' chatter and the clinking of expensive glassware filled the palatial home at least twice a month.

But on this quiet night, no crowds were present, just a contingent of dark-suited men with earpieces and slight gun bulges under their clothing. The men worked hard to remain inconspicuous around the house and property perimeter. Inside, Claire sat with Pamela Thatcher and a handful of associates near the fire in an alcove on the second story walkway that surrounded the two-story cherry wood library. French doors on each side of the fireplace led to a small portico that looked across a ten-acre pond, not quite frozen yet, to the moonlit silhouette of the Blue Ridge Mountains in the distance.

Over the mantel, a painting of the hunt forever reminded Claire of Aunt Pamela's years with her late husband Roland, of the vitality of his youthful efforts to build a benevolent post-War world, and of the rural, albeit affluent, peace and gentleness of their last decade together. More than anyone Claire had ever known, Uncle Roland could separate himself from the strife of daily life, penetrating deeply into the more tranquil mysteries of nature, whether skiing on a mountain slope, sailing into a stiff breeze, or sauntering on horseback through the woods surrounding Tidewater. He had been a man in touch with everything around him, surmounting every obstacle he encountered until a persistent cancer took him down in his final battle.

"I'm out of time," Joseph Mossoumou, president of the Middle African Democracy, said. A hulking presence with dark skin that distinguished him from the others in the room, Mossoumou drew on a large cigar and leaned into the antique mahogany table around which the group sat. The man's thick neck betrayed his personal physical disciplines. While the low, indirect lighting and dark woods predisposed the room to careful thought, Mossoumou no longer had any interest in contemplation. "I can't afford to wait any longer for all your chess pieces to align. MAD is about to explode. It's quickly getting down to kill or be killed." MAD was the commonly used acronym for Mossoumou's nation.

"Be patient, Joe," responded Tony Wayne, the US Under Secretary of State for African Affairs. Wayne sat between Pamela and Claire at the round table, directly opposite Mossoumou. He had roomed with the MAD leader at Harvard's JFK School of Government when they were both much younger. Wayne went on to leverage an early career in Foreign Service into a successful international law practice before joining the current administration. Mossoumou returned home to the Middle African Democracy (MAD), a former French colony. There, he worked hard within the government to build the prosperity of his people, only to watch it sucked away by AIDS and civil wars in the surrounding countries that were his primary trading partners. Nine years earlier, he had been elected President. He had been re-elected twice since, struggling day in and day out to both stem the tide of epidemic and establish trade with the stable west, a major challenge for a landlocked country in the middle of a continent with a lousy transportation infrastructure. His vision, more than his limited success, had resulted in Time Magazine declaring him the African continent's most important political leader.

"We're on track," Claire said to the group around the table. "Jennifer Winter just e-mailed confirmation that we should see production volumes of PDNAs from Prodeus next week. We'll be deployed before Christmas."

A tight grin broke Pamela Thatcher's grim demeanor. "Perfect," she said quietly.

"That's good news," Wayne said, sipping his single malt scotch. "It's teed up for you, Joe."

"Not good enough," Mossoumou said. "On schedule means a press conference after the New Year. We don't have that much time. MAD is pre-genocidal. Malaria and AIDS are killing my people by the tens of thousands each month. Productivity is dropping like a rock. We have some of the richest mineral deposits in the world, but we don't have the infrastructure and the funds to leverage enough of them to feed everyone. The hungrier everyone gets, the more desperate they get. Al Qaeda and other rebel groups are building momentum in the northeastern diamond fields. We already pushed them out once. It will be far more difficult a second time."

Pamela drummed her fingers on the table before speaking. "Once we're deployed in Sierra Leone, you'll have sea and air access. That should open a door for food, fuel and supplies."

"In January," Mossoumou said, his voice deep and his words evenly paced. "Assuming everything goes perfectly. Weeks matter. The press conference is the jumping off point, not the finish. January is too late."

"What if we could move the press conference up to Christmas or

Christmas Eve? Is that soon enough?"

"It's not ideal, but much better. My side of things will be ready."

Claire felt Pamela's eyes turn toward her. "My end will be ready, too," Claire said.

"I still would have preferred Nigeria," the MAD president said. "Much shorter supply line straight through Cameroon to the Nigerian delta."

"Not only is Nigeria an ally with a large standing army, Joe, but the HIV clade there has been identified for years," Pamela said. "The press and everyone else would see through our game pretty quickly if we tried it there. In Sierra Leone, the HIV type remains unknown. We've gone out of our way to keep it that way."

Claire sipped her club soda and lime before speaking. "Even if we went into Nigeria, both the vaccine program and the family planning initiative would be blocked by radical imams in the north and the Christian extremists in the south. We can control the geography and the data better in Sierra Leone."

"I agree," Under Secretary Wayne said. "Opening Sierra Leone clears access to the westernmost region of the Sierra Leone trench. Nailing down access and sea lanes from there to Equatorial Guinea lines up the largest and sweetest oil reserves on the planet."

"Short of Alberta," Mossoumou said.

Wayne sucked on his scotch before speaking. "We'd be hard-pressed to justify an invasion of Canada."

"Chinese are already investing heavily up there," Pamela said. "

"All the more reason to pin down West Africa," Wayne said. "Chinese would prefer to import their oil from West Africa rather than be dependent on American non-intervention in Canada. The plan gives us long-term leverage."

"I'm all in," Mossoumou said, his deep voice resonating. "Just don't leave me exposed. The Chinese have access to Sierra Leone's infrastructure. They won't part with it lightly."

Wayne sipped more scotch. "The Chinese do not have the military capability to reach halfway around the globe. They'll chalk it up to a lesson learned."

Pamela nodded agreement.

Claire sat back in her chair and watched the interaction. It impressed her how she and Pamela had taken the science the Aldrich developed and woven a fabric of genius from it. Plausible deniability was stamped all over the program. No official US government involvement. No oil company participation. Reporters and diplomats might scratch their heads, but ultimately they would attribute everything to the preparedness and brilliance of Joe Mossoumou in the face of a neighboring country's instability. Mossoumou had carefully engineered important cooperation in West and

Central Africa. The West wanted to love the MAD leader. His nation sat on the southern border of the Islamic north as well as east of the turmoil in West Africa. Nomadic herdsmen from neighboring Chad, funded by extreme Islamic interests out of the Sudan, threatened his northern border. Two MAD villages had been burned to the ground and over two thousand people massacred. MAD forces could only chase them to the border lest they give Chad and the Sudan an excuse to invade. Mossoumou said he had little doubt that the herdsmen intended to provoke just that.

But while Mossoumou's fight against radical Islam made him a media celebrity, his biggest potential contribution to the United States lie in his capacity for blocking Chinese economic influence and bringing long-term stability in the balkanized West African region – with a lot of help from Pamela, Claire and the Aldrich. Access to the port of Freetown would bring big benefits to landlocked MAD. Mossoumou and Thatcher had already sketched out a game plan for air freight from his capital to Freetown. Secretary Wayne, Mossoumou's old classmate, had provided assurances of a sea route protected by the US Navy from Freetown to Douala in Cameroon. US Army engineers already had surveyed an overland route from Douala to the heart of MAD, only about 800 miles, a manageable route for both trucks and tankers, and ultimately a pipeline to bring affordable oil to the landlocked nation.

"We have your back, Joe," Wayne said to Mossoumou. "A self-sufficient West Africa with the resources to both defend itself and build trade is in the best interests of both our countries. Minimizing the region's population pressures and driving up productivity are the formula for success."

Mossoumou pressed his lips together and sat back.

The under-secretary continued. "Disease presents our biggest challenge to productivity. Whack-a-mole with warlords is a close second. Both amount to a recipe for continued regional decline and further exploitation by the Chinese for the region's gold, oil and diamonds. So we're all about eradicating both disease and the warlords - quickly. We don't need another half century of tribal war and empire building in sub-Saharan Africa. And we don't need the Chinese establishing the region as a satellite."

Club soda in hand, Claire spoke, "AIDS and malaria could easily cause sub-Saharan Africa to fold in on itself independent of other issues."

Mossoumou took a long draw on his cigar. "The Chinese don't give a damn about the health of my region. Instability and dictators work well for them. They see the middle slice of my continent as an enormous and cheap land grab, from the Sudan in the east extending through my country in the center, going all the way to Sierra Leone in the west. We're not doing this out of some misguided ambition. We have no choice if we're to survive for the long run."

Mossoumou mesmerized Claire. He and Tony Wayne had been members of Pamela's circle for nearly twelve years. Claire watched them develop as she built her own credentials. While Wayne had become more and more of a bureaucrat, Joe had become even more of a true believer, impassioned about forging a better future for his people.

Wayne jiggled the remains of two ice cubes at the bottom of his empty scotch glass. "With the help of Claire and the Aldrich, we're going to get things going back in the right direction," he said. "Managing AIDS is the key. The economic cost of this damned scourge is unbearable. No country can prosper under these circumstances. Look at the official numbers for HIV infections now. Forty percent of the entire population of east equatorial Africa, fifteen percent and growing in West Africa."

"We'll prove AIDS can be managed in Sierra Leone," Claire said. "Beyond a shadow of a doubt."

Pamela added, "With your help, Joe."

"Just make sure I have the arms. And no issues with Nigeria. It's not clear that they're ready to concede their peacekeeping role in the region."

Pamela looked at Wayne. "No impediments here," the Under Secretary said. "Arms sales to MAD are completely unrestricted. And Nigeria is very pre-occupied with what amounts to civil war in the north. The nomadic herdsmen from Chad are giving them more fits than they ever gave MAD. Worse, the herdsmen are getting a sympathetic reception from the Islamic Nigerians that predominate the north." He turned to Mossoumou. "Looks like you did a nice job setting that up."

Mossoumou shrugged and said, "Our new friend in Libya took care of that. He's been pretty generous with contributions to the troublemakers. I imagine all he had to do was make some phone calls to get the nomads to move a few hundred miles west and annoy the Nigerians. For now."

"Tony, is there any reason to believe the White House will try to get in the way when Joe moves troops into Sierra Leone?" Pamela asked.

Wayne shook his head. "Not a chance. It's sub-Saharan Africa, Pamela. We have two military activities there: clandestine efforts in the ports and a drone operation in Niger to support the French in fighting Al Qaeda in Mali. Hell, the US African Command isn't even in Africa. It's in Stuttgart. The President knows the American public has no stomach for military action there. Americans, even most African Americans, don't spend too many cycles on African conflicts. That's traditionally British and French turf."

"What about the British?" Mossoumou asked.

"The British will welcome the help in Sierra Leone," Wayne said. "Plus they don't make a move without our blessing."

"Liberia?" Mossoumou pressed.

"Free for all. You can do what you want."

"Just don't get stupid," Pamela said. "Liberia's arguably Nigerian turf. We don't want to see you and the Nigerians slugging it out."

"She's right," Wayne added. "We need both of you. The White House might favor Nigeria in that situation. We like their oil."

"Your government needs me," Mossoumou said. "I hope the issue remains moot, but you might want to think about shifting the thinking to support MAD first. If I don't stay strong, political Islam moves south. Uncontained, nothing will stop their military ambitions. Nigeria has its own fundamentalist problems. There's no guarantee that they'll be good to you long-term."

After a moment, Pamela spoke, "So we proceed. We launch right after Thanksgiving. Claire, it's on your shoulders to make certain the malaria project is deployed."

"I'll make it happen," Claire said.

"And we're moving the press conference and all the elements surrounding it up to Christmas Eve."

Mossoumou ground out his cigar in the palm of his hand. He spoke quietly, "God help us."

The leader of Africa's fastest growing population stared into what was left of his now warm beer. Claire watched him and knew exactly what he wanted. He thought in terms of big picture and long term strategy over the lifetime of a culture, not individuals. He had no interest in slowing things down by wasting money and years beating back the raging brushfire that was AIDS. He wanted to kill it in a single blow. He wanted to accelerate the death rate and get it over with. Without bullets. Without armies.

And she had the weapon. President Mossoumou would like the CEM15-D problem.

She watched him reach into his pocket, certain he was feeling for the ancient Egyptian talisman he always carried. Claire even knew his mantra from Pamela's intelligence team. "Give me the strength of the Pharaohs," he allegedly intoned to himself. "And I will restore Africa to its glory."

Less than twenty minutes later, Mossoumou's head dropped to his chest and a sudden snore came out of his throat. Claire took it as a signal that the jet lag had caught up with him; while Nightline had not yet aired on the TV in Virginia, dawn would break shortly in central Africa. Pamela had Secretary Wayne's security detail help Mossoumou to one of the second floor guest rooms where he passed out for the night. Wayne and Claire did not trail far behind.

As Claire crawled under the covers, she slipped her reading glasses on. She made it through five pages of a distracting eBook fantasy on her phone when Pamela tapped on her door and entered dressed in a white nightgown.

Pamela sat on the edge of the bed near Claire's hips. She said nothing for a moment, only contemplated her hands.

Claire peered over her glasses. "Are you all right," she asked.

"That's what I came to ask you," Pamela responded.

"About what?"

Pamela held her gaze. Claire looked away. "Sheila? I just have to replace her," Claire said.

"With Jennifer?"

"Yes, but I have to get her back from Prodeus. She can pick up all the field work. Eldridge can double up on the lab issues."

"What about CEM15-D?"

"Sheila…" Claire started to choke up. "I'm sorry. I didn't think it would bother me like this."

Pamela placed a hand on her shoulder. "When the stakes are this high, our decisions can cut very deeply. You did what you had to do."

Claire took a few seconds to regain her composure. "Eldridge claims he can do it without her. Without Jennifer if need be."

"That's very risky. Just get her back. She's loyal. And she'll stay that way as long as she doesn't find out what happened with Sheila. She'll come back. She never really left, did she?"

"No, she's been our eyes and ears inside Prodeus."

"What about Dave Clement? Will he do what's needed if we take away his watchdog?"

"He's clueless about the subterfuge, Pamela. And now he has a very personal interest in our success."

"His daughter?"

"Right. Another tough decision. Who knew a man existed that couldn't be compromised by either a beautiful young woman or kickbacks? He left us no choice. Jennifer completed the first phase months ago. We hoped it would be enough to drive a wedge in the family and focus him on making money above all else. It turns out it wasn't. So we have to raise the stakes on him. Jennifer needs to finish the job before she comes back to the Aldrich."

"Ironic," Pamela said. "Clement's going to pay a dear price because he does the right thing. Makes you wonder who's really on the side of the angels — "

"We are," Claire said tersely. "Avenging angels."

Pamela leaned over Claire and stroked her hair. "Patience, love," she said. "So will Jennifer have a problem with the next phase?"

Claire felt herself relax as her aunt slowly ran her fingers back and forth through her hair, just as Pamela had done when she sat by her side in the hospital decades earlier. "She always knew it was a possibility," Claire said. "But I don't think she ever thought she'd fail to compromise him with her charms."

Pamela's eyes lit up. "Is he gay? Or asexual?"

"Neither," Claire said, "Our surveillance proved he has a very healthy appetite for his wife."

Pamela shrugged. "I don't want to know how you know that. Technology is helpful, but I swear it disgusts me at times."

"We do what we have to do."

"Jennifer's a very beautiful young woman," Pamela continued. "Must have been a blow to her ego. I suppose Dave's just a different animal. A throwback."

"To what? Men have always been pigs. He's just an anomaly."

"Don't be so bitter, Joanne -"

Claire's face reddened and her eyes glared. "Never call me that. Joanne is gone. You of all people know better."

"My mind jumped back twenty years. Sorry." She waited while Claire's anger subsided.

"Sorry I reacted so strongly," Claire said after a moment, the flush in her cheeks dissipating.

"It's okay. I understand. Bitterness doesn't help, though. When this is over, you're going to feel very different."

"You're right," Claire answered. "I'm going to feel like I've finally buried Joanne once and for all."

"I hope so, love."

Claire rolled on to her side, facing away from her aunt. Pamela remained the only person with whom Claire felt comfortable showing herself this way.

Pamela began massaging her back. Claire purred. "That feels nice. I remember when you would rub ointment on my back every night," she said. "Just thinking about that puts me to sleep some nights."

"You're a very spoiled girl."

"I know." Claire shifted her hips and slid toward the middle of the bed. "Do you trust President Mossoumou?" she asked.

"Absolutely not," Pamela replied. "Joe has an enormous ego and a messiah complex. By his very nature, he's quite treacherous. But also very predictable."

"Tony Wayne's big boss won't like that kind of risk."

"Our President wants to get a lock on West African crude. He'll learn to live with it."

Claire enjoyed the massage for a moment before another doubt rushed through her mind. "Do Mossoumou and Tony Wayne really understand how many people could die before we stabilize the medicine?"

The rhythm of Pamela's massage continued without disruption. "They didn't get where they were by being short-sighted," she answered. "They know the long term math heavily favors our strategy."

Pamela picked a knotted muscle just below Claire's right shoulder blade and pressed in very slowly with a gentle kneading action. Claire closed her eyes momentarily before they flapped open again.

"Before I get too peaceful, any other news?" Claire said.

"I knew you couldn't let it go. Not even for one night."

"Could you?"

"I haven't." Pamela said.

"So?"

"Steady progress. Holy Mother Church is really a very simple thing to manage once you understand its combination of bureaucracy and naiveté."

"And treachery," added Claire.

"And treachery," confirmed Pamela.

As she drifted off, Claire thought of her mother on that gray day, dressed in white, smiling and happy with her family. She saw her baby sister, too. She adored that child. Reflected in the passenger windows of a dark sedan, Claire glimpsed herself, as yet unsullied by the life that followed, cooing at her baby sister. No price paid would be too dear for what happened in the moments that followed.

Then, in her dreams, she saw Liv Clement's face super-imposed on her reflection. Her mother, somehow returned to life, wrapped her in her arms on the damp Belfast sidewalk all those years ago. She felt a oneness with Liv, felt her innocence as strong as the innocence she knew in herself at that age. Then white light filled her dream. Searing heat overwhelmed her as enormous pressure threatened to make her head explode. In the blinding light, she found herself reaching for her mother and her sister, but she could not find them.

Claire awoke trembling in the black night of the bedroom. For a brief moment, she did not know where she was. Gradually, the nightmare faded and the terror subsided as her eyes adjusted to the darkness. She was alone. Pamela had long since retreated to her own bedroom. Claire pulled the blanket up to her chin and rolled on to her side.

"Dad, help me to see this through," she whispered into the dark. She felt no response. Instead, she felt completely alone. She hugged her pillow. The empty void around her mushroomed into a desolate wasteland of endless blackness. No hands reached out to comfort. No God existed to render hope. A profound fear gripped her, squeezing her heart so tight that she gasped for breath.

"Dad," she pleaded. "I miss you." She still did not feel a response. She steeled herself, slowly taking deep breaths.

"By Christmas," she said. "I promise. We will make them pay."

Pulling the covers tighter, she drew her knees up toward her chest as though to make herself smaller. She prayed for dreamless sleep that did not come.

Public Offerings continues in

Public Offerings Book Three:
Killer Priest

Enjoy the free excerpt that follows

Learn more at www.PublicOfferings.net

Follow at www.Facebook.com/PublicOfferings

EXCERPT:

PUBLIC OFFERINGS BOOK THREE:

KILLER PRIEST

CHAPTER 1

Fort Collins: Clement Home
November 24, 9:25 p.m. Mountain Time

The emptiness. The nagging fear of loss. They scratched at his soul like thorns slowly dragged up and down. But more than his soul ached. The hollow pain touched him physically, relentlessly.

Finally home. Finally able to spend time with his daughter after months away. Then an hour ago, he undermined everything. Fussed at her for no good reason. Because she wanted to spend time alone. He thought she wanted to be away from him. He wanted her to just sit down with him. Watch television. Play Clue or Monopoly. Anything to be together. But Liv just wanted to be by herself, perfectly normal for a fifteen year old, especially one wrestling with a deadly illness. Why couldn't he understand that?

In the middle of his minor eruption, Mel told him to back down. He told her not to get between "me and my daughter."

"Don't undermine me, Mel," he said to his wife under his breath.

"What's with your attitude?" he demanded of Liv. "I just want you to spend some time down here with us. You're all pouts and snorts. And short answers. I'm sick and tired of your short answers. You have no respect. Do you realize the sacrifices I make for you?"

She just stared at him, curled back into her chair, her body turned away from him, tears building in reddening eyes.

"Not that I mind the sacrifices," he continued. "Not that I mind breaking my ass. But I do mind when it's for an ingrate. At least you can show a little respect. Spend a little time with us. Instead, you'd rather hide up in your room, feeling sorry for yourself. Or texting your friends. I'll take your phone away and pull the plug on that damned computer if you don't straighten up."

As his explosion of comments ended their string, he started to hear himself. Started to see that he had frightened Liv, hurt her. Pushed her away when all he wanted to do was draw her closer. She had no idea that she had hurt him. He was Dad, the guy who could always take care of himself and everyone else. She just wanted him home. Wanted to know he was there. She had argued with her mother over it. Now, he had turned on her. Angrily. Hatefully. She felt certain that he hated her.

He recognized all that in the pain in her eyes. He recognized it in her determination not to let tears pour out, tears that brimmed on her eyelids, crying that caused the muscles to tremor around her half-open pout.

"Can I go upstairs now?" she asked in a quiet voice after a thirty second break in her father's tirade.

Mel looked at Dave. He could not answer.

"Yes," she answered for him. "Give us a kiss good night."

Liv bent down and kissed her mother.

"I love you, Liv," Mel said, pressing her hands on the side of her daughter's head.

Liv started to walk by Dave's chair.

"Liv," Mel said.

Liv turned and kissed her father on the forehead.

"I love you, too, Liv," he said.

"Okay," she mumbled.

She went up the stairs. Dave stared at his hands for a moment. "Dear God, Mel. What's wrong with me?"

"You tell me," she quietly demanded.

"I want to be with her more than anything in the world. She and you. Sometimes, she's the only thing that gives me peace."

"Me, too. Please, please, don't undermine that."

"I'm sorry. Will you talk to her?"

"Let's give her some time to deal with it herself. She did lip off. And she has been rude. But you overreacted."

He felt an urge to argue, but found no basis other than pride. "I agree," he said. "Lord knows, she has more to be stressed about than any other kid her age. At least, around here."

"We shouldn't just let the attitude go, though. But we shouldn't treat her like a serial killer either."

"I feel so damned horrible. The poor kid. She's been so strong through all this garbage."

Mel tilted her head slightly and looked hard at him. "Stop beating yourself up, Dave. She'll get over it. And you'll get plenty of time to show her you love her. One person feeling sorry for herself around here is enough."

Now he stood alone on the back deck as Fort Collins' autumn chill knocked temperatures down into the low 40s. As he started to shiver, a product of anxiety as much as the air temperature, he folded his arms to ward off the cold. Mel had gone upstairs to console Liv. He awaited her return with a verdict.

He stared at the sky, at the limitless expanse of space. He noticed how empty it felt amidst those billions of stars, how he related only to the darkness and not the distant twinkling glimmers – related to the void. And he feared the void, the hard, hard emptiness of a world without Liv. He only wanted to feel her warmth tonight, hold her like he did when she was still so little, her head tucked into the small of his neck, her hand warm in his, his soul calmed and peaceful, his heart knowing that he brought tranquil security to her, enfolding her in his love, protecting her from that very void.

Tonight, he had launched her into the void all alone. Launched her with his desperation just when she needed him most. She would get over it by morning, leave it behind as one of the quirks of parenthood. Mel assured him of that when she finally returned downstairs after what seemed a lifetime.

It would be different for him. He would always worry about the damage done short and long-term to her self-worth by the degrading tape he drilled into her head.

He would never forget.

CHAPTER 2

Rome: Ignatian College
November 25, 8:45 a.m. Central European Time

Lovers and tourists crowded the steep Spanish Steps just up the street from the Trevi Fountain where the same lovers might make a wish and toss a coin over their shoulder. Around the corner in an eight-story building covered in ancient plaster and shuttered windows, a group of twelve men met in the dining room of the Ignatian College's residence hall.

The interior of the building belied its plain exterior of thick plastered stone walls. Entering from the noisy hustle and bustle of Rome's hectic streets, a crescendo of quiet besieged the visitor as the heavy oak doors closed behind him. In the center of the building, Italian hawk moths, similar from a distance in appearance and behavior to American hummingbirds, hovered over lavender blooms in a fragrant open courtyard filled with tall junipers and bright flowers.

In a gloomy dining room of tapestries and elaborately carved wood, the ancient furnishings and dark paneling absorbed the final word on much of the information discussed and exchanged. The Apostles of Christus knew that anything less than complete secrecy might alter both their earthly and eternal destinies.

The chairman, a slender man in the red cassock of a cardinal, stirred his tea as he began. "Good fathers, it appears the devil is raising the stakes. We have urgent news from the United States this morning. A priest from our society called the US center warning of a genocidal plan birthed in the mountains of Colorado. Within hours of his call, someone stabbed him to death outside his rectory in Pittsburgh."

He paused and rubbed the side of his long aquiline nose with his manicured index finger. Watching the faces, he waited until the group had absorbed his words. He sipped his tea, peering over the rim of his cup. He continued, "There is strong evidence that a splinter IRA faction is in the middle of this, running security for the operation. Information provided by the murdered pastor aligns with innuendo gathered from pastoral counseling over the last few months."

A young monsignor, destined for much higher office in the church, leaned forward to be seen. An American, Stan Zabinski came from a well-to-do Chicago family. Such men rarely came to the church these days. Different stakeholders within the Vatican bureaucracy all wanted a piece of him, but Christus had won out.

The loss of his fiancé in the World Trade Center bombing in 2001 had affected him deeply, ultimately altering his life plan. On a three-month internship with a brokerage firm there, Patricia called him back in Chicago twice a day expressing how much she missed him and how homesick she was for Chicago. She did not work in the World Trade Center, but had, after months of persistence, secured a job interview there with one of the biggest bond traders on the globe. That morning, she called Stan from the lobby of the North Tower, getting one last pep talk from him before taking the elevator to the 98th floor. She told Stan she loved him and that she could not wait to see him back home in Chicago in just two days. The 8 a.m. interview was supposed to last only 30 minutes. But the interviewer must have been impressed because she was still there when the first plane came in at 8:46. It would be ten weeks before they identified her body in the rubble.

At first he cursed God, completely immersing himself in his work at an investment banking firm, but months of sleepless nights drove him into downtown Chicago's Holy Name Cathedral one morning. Dropping to his knees beneath the massive Romanesque arches of the church, he began an earnest conversation with the Lord. He started praying to be rid of his anger, but then realized he did not need God to end his anger, but instead to help him know at whom to be angry. Jesus, after all, showed anger at the moneychangers in the Temple. It felt like a breakthrough to Zabinski. But he knew the anger and the deep hatred building inside him could not serve God unless he channeled it constructively. He wrote a letter to the Trib in response to an editorial portraying the Afghan invasion and the plan to eradicate Al Qaeda as a panacea for what happened at the World Trade Center. He wrote that poverty, desperation and power provided fertile ground for despots like Osama Bin Laden to build their radical visions. Eliminating that desperation and its breeding grounds, he wrote, presented the only real hope for an ultimate end to terrorism and its champions.

The Trib published the letter. Then, twelve days later, he received a call from an aid to Pamela Thatcher. The great lady herself planned to be in Chicago. Did he have time to meet with her? He did. And that meeting opened his eyes and re-directed his course.

Less than a year later, he matriculated in a seminary. Six years of prior undergraduate and graduate school fast-tracked him there. He also had spent a year as superintendent for one of his father's shopping center developments between undergrad and business school. The hardball of the metro Chicago construction business grounded him in strong street-level experience to complement his academic training. And throughout his time in seminary, he knew Pamela Thatcher kept an eye on him. Contributions from wealthy donors, attributed to his work as an assistant pastor in inner city Chicago, led to his coming to the attention of the leaders of the Church all the way to Rome. A whispered campaign within the hierarchy touted his background and experience, fast-tracking him to assignment in Rome and ultimately his selection by the Apostles of Christus.

"The news is very disturbing, eminence," Monsignor Zabinski said. "So what's the bottom line?

The cardinal bowed his head over his teacup, organizing his thoughts before speaking. "We know," he said, slowly lifting his head, "that there is very likely a plot afoot to commit genocide via some kind of genetic intervention. What we don't know is specifically how that will happen."

"There is one thing of utmost interest," said Father Adam, a trusted American septuagenarian with a slight southern accent and a perpetual smell of cigarettes on his clothes. "This latest information triangulates with rumors we have been hearing for some time, rumors we could not act on because many came in veiled messages culled from the confessional. But…"

Father Adam looked hard at Zabinski. "…we know that IRA extremists went to Colorado months ago to protect a research site of some kind. This may be the site in question."

The chair grew impatient. "So how do we get inside this research site?"

"That, eminence, I cannot answer."

"But you do have the answer, Father Adam," Monsignor Zabinski interrupted.

Adam turned to face Zabinski. "I don't understand."

"Our miracle man from Sierra Leone."

The cardinal and the priests knew immediately who the miracle man was. Though kept out of the press, Fr. Jim Reilly's dramatic return to Rome quickly became legend in the halls of the Vatican. Many insiders considered his survival in a coffin over 9 hours at high altitude to be nothing less than direct intervention from heaven. While the kidnappers thought he would survive, scientists consulted by the Vatican said the kidnappers clearly lacked an understanding of what happens to oxygen in that environment. Fr. Jim should have died en route. Vatican priests of all ranks, often embittered and hardened by the politics and administrivia of the Catholic Church's immense bureaucracy, found respite from their anger and ambitions in the miracle of the Irish missionary.

Fr. Adam tensed. "Don't," he said to Zabinski.

"He's no longer your student, Father," the Monsignor said. "The Church needs him. Don't you think the Lord saved him for a reason?"

"I should never have told you. I confided in you as friend and confessor."

"And when I recruited you to join Christus here in Rome, the Holy Spirit laid down a path I could not have foreseen," Zabinski responded. "Fr. Jim doesn't need your protection any more. The Lord has good hold of him."

Zabinski leaned back and scanned the room. "The IRA faction in Colorado," he said. "The one we think may guard the secrets of the genocide – its leader is an old IRA hand named Michael Farley."

Adam's face paled, his jaw slackening as his eyes widened.

"Fr. Adam, do you want to tell them?" Zabinski continued.

"Mike Farley is Fr. Jim's brother," Father Adam said quietly.

"Fr. Reilly's brother?" the cardinal asked looking back and forth at the two men.

Zabinski explained. "Jim Reilly is an alias assumed when the man we know as Fr. Reilly turned his back on the IRA life to enter the seminary. His birth name was Sean Farley. Priests in Ireland have easy access to birth and death certificates, y'know."

The priests around the table leaned in a little further. Only the Lord could provide such a "coincidence." A few blessed themselves with the sign of the cross.

"What's your connection to this man, Father?" The cardinal asked Fr. Adam.

Adam folded his hands and contemplated them before lifting his head and speaking. "He's very special to me. Like a son. He escaped IRA thugs in Ireland as a child. I protected him as my student in the monastery in Georgia for many years."

The cardinal smiled. "Then your charity has blessed us. The Lord saw today's problems coming far in advance. Through you, he prepared part of our solution. Decades ago."

"I hope you're right, Eminence," Fr. Adam said.

"Are the brothers still in touch with one another?" the cardinal asked.

"As Father Adam can tell you, they haven't spoken in years," Zabinski explained. "Fr. Jim Reilly prays every day for his brother Mike to repent. The brother, on the other hand, waits for the priest to tire of holy rollers and return to the field of combat."

"Reilly never really left it, did he?" the cardinal asked rhetorically. "From what I hear, he seems drawn to trouble spots."

"He did leave his own violence behind," Zabinski said. "By his own choice, he has been a missionary in the roughest spots on the globe. And he is completely non-violent."

Father Adam interrupted, "He has given almost every moment to our Lord since he was twelve. Through his guilt, he struggles hard to find God's peace. If anyone can, his brother could destroy that hope for peace once and for all. Fr. Jim's soul would be at risk."

The cardinal focused hard on the old man. "Would he kill again, Father? If he needed to save others. Does he have the will to defend himself and others with lethal force?"

Fr. Adam slowly shook his head from side to side. "I don't really know. I'm certain it's the last thing he wants to face. Jim lives a life of perpetual penance, more so than anyone else I have ever known. He may stand up so bravely to danger because part of him wants to make amends by being martyred."

"So would he pull the trigger or just stand there and die?" Zabinski pressed.

"He would let the Holy Spirit guide him at that moment."

"Let's hope the Holy Spirit talks fast if he should find himself in that situation. In the extreme, the fate of millions could rely on him to transcend his piety and self-pity."

Fr. Adam's face reddened. "Would you have him kill his own brother?" the priest countered.

Zabinski spoke without hesitation, "Of course. We're all brothers. His mission is to help the entire brotherhood of mankind."

"Enough, gentlemen," the cardinal interrupted. "Argument enough for me is that we have been provided by inexplicable miracle with the brother of this enemy. The Lord has singled out Fr. Jim Reilly. It is not for us to fathom the reasons, only to be obedient to God's will."

Twenty minutes later, Zabinski dropped into the chair behind his desk at the Vatican. He pressed his fingers to his forehead. Rage churned inside him as he thought about the hypocritical saintly posturing of some of the ambitious men at the meeting. The pompous pious, he thought. As if an almighty Creator would waste his time on their churchy details. They would learn the price of their misplaced trust. They would learn who provided this "inexplicable miracle."

Smug self-satisfaction replaced rage inside him. Pamela will be pleased, he thought.

CHAPTER 3

Boulder, Colorado: Aldrich Institute
November 26, 7:50 a.m. Mountain Time

Claire's face burned crimson.

"What does she know? How the hell did she find out in the first place?"

She listened as the person on the other end of the phone connection explained himself in a thick Irish brogue.

"You don't go to Walden, Colorado, by accident, Farley," she said heatedly.

She drummed her fingers on the desk as the man continued to explain himself.

"Look, I hired you people because I thought you knew what you were doing," Claire said. "Did she identify the body for the police?"

She nodded as she listened. "Good. That's our girl. Always a team player."

Her eyes widened as a she listened to the man's proposal. "No. Absolutely not. Don't you dare. She did not identify the body. If she was working against us, she would have told that cop. She knew enough to leave it be. I'll take it from here myself. Jennifer can be trusted. She just needs to understand."

She listened as the man concurred, apparently happy to get the monkey off his back.

"Good, we're in agreement. I'll let you know if anything goes wrong."

She hung up without even saying good-bye. She opened her favorites on her phone and tapped Jennifer's name.

"Jennifer? It's Claire."

In her cubicle at Prodeus, Jennifer's eyes widened when she saw the caller ID on her mobile phone. She quickly walked to an empty conference room and closed the door before answering.

"What's up, Claire?" Jennifer struggled to sound casual as she slid into a chair at the conference room table. She had been Claire's biggest defender. Now, she suspected her of having Sheila murdered. Sheila had replied to Jennifer's e-mail at one Friday morning from her desk in the lab, the only place Sheila had e-mail access because the mountain lab prohibited the use of mobile phones for both email and texting for security reasons.

Yet a housekeeper found her body in a motel room in Walden early Friday morning. How and why did she go to Walden between 1 a.m. and 9 a.m.? Jennifer knew she would not have gone willingly. Something happened in the lab that night.

"I'm calling to see if you're okay," Claire said.

"I'm good. You?"

"Sheila left us."

She knows that I know, Jennifer thought. Claire always seemed to know everything. "That's a blow to our effort," Jennifer said.

"Probably never hear from her again. I don't think she was very happy with some of our decisions on the mountain."

Jennifer had to be careful. If Claire did have Sheila killed, the same fate could be in store for Jennifer if she let on that she knew about it. Any form of disloyalty might risk a death penalty.

"Look, Jennifer. I'll cut to the chase."

Jennifer tapped the end of a pen on her desk as she listened.

"We need you back at the Aldrich. You're our best hope to fill in for Sheila."

Jennifer stopped tapping her pen. Her mouth went dry and she felt herself shrivel inside. She could not go back into the lab. That would make her as vulnerable as Sheila. "No, Claire. Find someone else. I have a good deal here. When Prodeus goes public, I'm going to make more money than I ever dreamed of."

"Jennifer. Do you hear yourself? Have you lost sight of the big picture? You helped architect it."

Jennifer's hand tightened around the pen. "I helped with a plan to save lives, not take them."

"I don't know what you think you know, but you don't anything about what has to be done. We will be saving lives for generations."

"I can't do it, Claire. I can't leave. My future's here now. That was the plan of record last time I looked." Jennifer rolled the pen between her fingers.

"If you're counting on a public offering of Prodeus stock, I won't let that happen. You'll make your money with us."

"Not a very good idea," Jennifer said.

"You'll be safe here. Think about it."

"I feel safe at Prodeus." The pen snapped in her grip.

"Make this easy. You don't have a choice. It's my decision. You and the boys at Prodeus exist because I let you exist. I can change that in a minute."

Jennifer quivered as she watched the ink run over her fingers. "Why are you threatening me? I've only been loyal to you."

"I'm not threatening. I'm imploring you. The Aldrich mission is bigger than both of us. We need to do what's best for everyone."

"I'm not going back."

Claire did not respond right away. Jennifer tucked the phone between her chin and her shoulder to hold it while she grabbed a tissue from her purse. She wiped her hand while she waited, trying not to be frantic.

"And what about the next step with the Clements?" Claire asked. "Will you do what you have to do, what you committed you would do if necessary?"

The tissue only smeared the ink on Jennifer's hand. She reached for more, but knocked the tissue box to the floor. When she reached for it, her phone dropped to the floor. Balling her hands into fists, she felt like screaming. Taking deep breaths, she calmed herself and picked up the phone.

"Neither one of us ever really believed it would come to that, Claire," she said.

"We both did."

"I didn't. They're good people."

"What we're doing is bigger than a few good people. With Sheila gone, the outcome's ultimately in your hands. You can break it. And you can fix it."

"If I come back to the Aldrich, I can fix it. But so can Eldridge. I won't do it. Not now. And I won't break anything else for you. I've done enough already."

Claire said nothing.

"You have to understand," Jennifer said. "We're doing this to help people, not hurt them. That's how you taught us."

Still nothing from Claire.

"Please don't do this to me, Claire." This time, Jennifer waited for Claire to say something. She looked at the second hand on the wall clock in the conference room. She watched it tick off 40 seconds and felt like she did not breathe the entire time.

Finally, Claire spoke. "I'm sure you'll re-consider."

The phone clicked as Claire hung up. Jennifer rolled the chair away from the conference table and hunched over, grabbing her legs behind the knees and shaking like a leaf. At times like these, she wished she still had some kind of religion. Who could she turn to? She couldn't very well call her mother in Texas with this one.

Picking up her briefcase, she left the building, reassuring herself that she would be back. She walked to the parking lot in a surrealistic daze. Someone had murdered her closest friend and her mentor had fundamentally just threatened her. Trembling, she dropped her keys on the floor of the car three times before finally shoving them in the ignition.

CHAPTER 4

Freetown: Outside refugee camp
November 26, 3:10 p.m. Greenwich Mean Time

Dust filled the air as the crowd, smelling of sweat and old fruit, gathered around the journalists near the camp's small makeshift market at the main gate. The markets' stalls were lean-to's made of cracked, rotten wood. Scavenged from the remains of buildings destroyed in the fighting in town, the wood formed jigsaw puzzles of irregular shapes nailed together in creative necessity. The items offered by vendors included fruit picked from the nearby jungle, children's clothing items that had been outgrown by the vendors' children, and fresh wood for cooking chopped from a now nearly defoliated field south of the camp. Some of the items, like the rice cooked at a small stand that sold handfuls of it, had been carried in by arriving refugees in the manner traditional in the region: on their heads.

Mariama Karanja, wearing a loose-fitting dark green caftan that kept slipping off her shoulders, stayed back from the journalists and the pleaders surrounding them. Her grip tightened on the hand of three-year-old daughter Emma. She kept her away from crowds, fearful that the close contact might weaken her immune system. That could either make her sick like Sara or make her unable to visit Sara for fear of worsening Sara's condition.

The little girl shuffled her pink plastic sandals in the dust as her mother coaxed her to a shady spot made available by the crowd's rush to tell stories to the journalists. Two slender twin trunks, reaching high above the camp's security fencing, cast flimsy but welcome shade between two of the lean-tos. Many of the native trees had been bulldozed to make room for the camp. Enterprising refugees who sold logs for fuel had long since chopped down those of any substance that remained unscathed by the original clearing effort. The leafy tree over Mariama and Emma had likely survived because of its anorexic trunk and branches.

"You get over here, woman!"

Appearing suddenly from behind the ramshackle medical clinic, the man wore a soiled white t-shirt and khaki shorts. He sucked on a beer can, the foam dribbling down the curly, black stubble on his unshaven chin.

"Where the hell are you?" he shouted. Spotting the object of his rage, he plowed into the crowd. He re-surfaced a moment later, pulling a small woman behind him. Neither came from the Karanjas' village.

"I expected my rice by now. You are a wife. You will do as I ask."

"Let me go, you pig," she yelled, swatting at him.

He slammed her in the back with his forearm and she stumbled to the ground. He kicked her repeatedly in the side, yelling for her to get up.

The frightened Emma clung to her mother, but Mariama knew she could not let the man keep beating his wife. Bending down to her daughter's ear, Mariama said, "You wait here and hold on to this tree, Emma. I have to help that woman."

"No, mama. Don't. He'll hurt you."

Mariama pressed a finger on her daughter's lips and smiled gently. She then turned and walked over to stand beside the cowering woman.

"Sir, leave her be," Mariama demanded, standing up straight with her hands on her hips.

"You be gone, lady, before I do the same to you."

"You don't want to be doing this, Mister."

"The hell you say. This is a private matter."

The man kicked his wife again. Mariama stepped over the woman and into the face of the man.

"If you want to kick someone, you can kick me, Mister. My husband is a paramount chief. Kick me and our entire village will be your enemy."

The man turned his face away, taking another swig of his beer. He used a forearm to wipe sweat off his unshaven face. He faced Mariama now, his eyes widening and his chest swelling with fresh rage.

"Mama!" Emma screamed and ran toward the man.

At the same time, the man swung his beer can around and slammed it into Mariama. Warned by Emma's scream, she ducked just enough to receive the first blow on the shoulder instead of the face. As his next blow came down toward her head, his hips suddenly caved in and he stumbled over the prone, sobbing body of his wife. He fell backward over her. Emma stood huffing on the spot from which she had pushed him. The man started to get back up and the little girl ran into her mother's arms.

He reached down, picked up his wife and threw her to the side. Turning to Mariama, he yelled, "You and your little brat are dead!" He stepped over to a fruit vendor and grabbed his knife. Waving the knife, he charged at Mariama. A faint crack echoed in the distance. Blood exploded from the man's neck, his momentum thrusting him at Mariama's feet. More gunfire followed and the crowd scattered. Mariama and Emma ran toward the infirmary. As they did, the little girl blessed herself. Uncertain as to who was shooting who, Mariama did likewise.

From behind an abandoned car outside the main gate, Jacob took careful aim one more time, but the man did not get back up. Jacob could not let the rest of his family die. They were victims of Hamara's betrayal, just as he was. It was for Hamara and the other village chiefs they had come. For weeks, his commanders drummed into him the story that Hamara had betrayed his people. In his drug-induced state, Jacob became convinced it was true. Today, he again carried an AK-47, given one more chance to prove himself to the thugs that had become his masters.

Using a pick-up truck 20 yards behind Jacob for cover, the teenaged commander yelled, "Go now! Go! Go!"

Fifteen young boys ran toward the gate, rifles nearly as big as them swinging at their sides. Jacob held back. They were to hit and run, returning to the jungle and then coming back again at a different spot, each time firing into the camp for effect.

"What are you doing?" he called to the commander. "This is suicide!"

The teenager, uniformed in a black Nike t-shirt and Old Navy skater shorts, pointed his pistol toward Jacob. "I am the commander here, boy. You do as I say or this time I'll do more than just take away your rifle."

Jacob had seen the teenager kill ruthlessly before. He got up from his knees and ran toward the camp. He mumbled a quick prayer that the Lord protect him and then he started screaming like the other boys.

Several armed men suddenly appeared at the gate. They were camp constabulary, meant to keep order within the camp, not fight rebel units. The boys fired inaccurately while on the run, giving the men inside time to aim. Two boys fell in front of Jacob. He dodged them and ran to the side, taking cover behind a trash dumpster.

From behind safe cover, the young commander and the three other teenagers he brought with him yelled at the boys to keep going, but several of the boys had turned to run away. As one of the retreating boys ran past the pick-up truck where the teens took cover, the commander fired at him, dropping the boy instantly.

The remaining boys reversed course again, yelling that the commander was killing them. One of them fell to fire from the camp.

Jacob peered through his scope and squeezed. A red hole appeared in the rebel commander's forehead, his eyes still wide open as he fell forward. The other three teens looked around in confusion. They did not know where the shot came from.

Jacob fired again. Another teen fell. Now the other younger boys, all pinned down behind varying forms of cover from palm trees to trash piles, watched Jacob. They saw what he was doing. Several of them now turned their rifles in the same direction as Jacob's was pointed. The remaining teens died in a flurry of bullets.

"Follow me!" Jacob yelled as he ran up the hill into the jungle.

Confused by what they had seen, the constabulary held their fire while they watched the boys run off.

Back in the jungle, Jacob rallied the boys in the deep foliage. They were all panting, all frightened.

"We have no friends," he said. "And now we can't go back to the rebels."

"We can say the commander and his friends were killed by the constabulary," one of the boys suggested.

"Even if they believe us and even if one of you doesn't tell, how long do you think it will be before another stupid commander asks us to kill ourselves?" Jacob said. "Look what just happened. They don't care about us. They use us."

Consensus quickly surfaced among the group. Though Jacob had become their peer leader, one of them suggested formally electing him their captain. All but three of the surviving 11 boys voted for him.

"So, sir, Chief Karanja still lives," one of the dissenters said, his tone surly. "Will we return to the camp to finish our job and kill him?"

Jacob glared at the boy and then grabbed him by the hair. "No. Did you see those guns? They're ready for us. We need to be smarter about where we attack."

"All I want is food and a good place to sleep," said another boy.

Jacob peered at him and then back at the boy he had by the hair. "Any other questions?" he said.

Obstinate with his pride on the line now, the boy challenged, "What about your father?"

"He's my business," Jacob fumed. "Mine only."

Suddenly, the now familiar drug-fired rage rose inside him. He hefted his rifle into the air and hit the boy in the head with the stock.

Another boy moved toward Jacob to keep him from striking again. Jacob turned toward him, his angry eyes discouraging the boy from taking another step. On the ground, the first boy moaned, blood matting on the side of his head.

Jacob crouched beside him. "I heard that moan," he said. "I guess that means you've changed your vote."

The other boys laughed nervously, even the wounded dissenter.

CHAPTER 5

Prodeus: Ed Hepp's office
November 26, 8:45 a.m. Mountain Time

Chunky forearms lay across his desk in front of him, beefy fingers interlaced in folded hands to hide their tremors, Ed Hepp peered over the top of his bi-focals at Dave. Behind him rolled the pastoral backdrop of a snow-covered horse pasture and the white-capped peaks of the Front Range.

"I'm going to do you a favor, Dave. How about I authorize you to get rid of one of your biggest headaches? What if I tell you I want you to fire Jennifer Winter?"

Dave lifted a disbelieving eyebrow. "How's that a favor? She's an enormous asset."

"She's a pain in the butt and you know it. C'mon, Dave. It's no secret that she's got a thing for you. Can't be comfortable."

Dave's face turned pale. "What's that have to do with keeping her or not?"

"You two were seen in the boardroom after the impromptu meeting last week. I'm told that you were very clear in saying no."

"How were we seen?"

Ed threw his beefy hands up and looked to the ceiling. "The door was open. You think the employees around here don't follow the execs like we're celebrities. Of course, they do. And Dave..." He leaned forward and whispered, "Jennifer's little escapades with you make for great stories."

"I can't believe this. So we're going to fire the kid because she came on to me."

Ed contorted his face. "No. I thought that would be an enticement, though. You're firing her because she pissed off Claire McQuaid. And the main justification for her existence has been her relationship with Claire."

Dave's belly gnawed at him. His call to Claire did this. He protected Sheila, but underestimated Claire's ability to reach into Prodeus. Claire did not want him or anyone to know about the Aldrich HIV research. She was delivering a message to both Dave and Jennifer while closing the door on Liv. He slipped back in his seat and looked out the window past Ed.

"How will we cover her work for the launch?"

The additional workload and disruption risked by her departure would be both stressful and risky, he thought. And thus far, Sheila had not found a way to get the password to him for her newest cloud folder. Jennifer could be his only line on that. Dave felt certain she knew more than she had already said.

"Hire somebody else."

"We're not going to find someone and train him or her in a few weeks. Jennifer gets this stuff. She understands the code, the statistics, and the trial guidelines."

"So do you."

"I don't have enough hours in the day as it is."

"Find them."

And kiss my marriage good-bye once and for all, he thought. It would be months before he could do more than catch a few hours' sleep at home. "Did Claire say why she was pissed?"

"Said Jennifer's too pig-headed, that she almost killed the negotiations last month. She complimented you, by the way. You, my friend, are the reason that she rolled over for us."

"Ed," he said, looking back to his boss, "that's not the way it was at all..."

"Dave? I'm surprised you're fighting me on this. Sounds like maybe you really do having something going with Jennifer."

"Hell, no. She's just an important asset around here. We can't afford to lose her. Not now."

"McQuaid is pissed with her. Middleton can't stand her. She's trying to wreck your marriage. Am I missing something?"

Dave exhaled in exasperation. "Yes, Ed. You are."

"Mind telling me what?"

"I do. I do mind."

"Unless you plan to fire her, you don't have a lot of choice."

Dave's mind whirled. Ed's heavy-handedness had him seething. He tried to calm himself, to think this through. Whether he fired her or not, McQuaid's attitude would ultimately push Jennifer out. Unless Dave just stood by her. How would that look? If Mel even had a clue about Jennifer's come-on's, odds on keeping the marriage intact imploded. Not to mention that she would kill him for not firing her when he had the chance. And if he did fire her, Mel would be all over him for living at the office and on the road. A complete no-win situation. But, with Sheila not communicating, Jenn's insight on the prospect of a cure for Liv would trump with Mel. That would transcend everything – if Jennifer was telling the truth.

So Jennifer ends up on the street for her apparent willingness to risk her relationship with McQuaid to help Liv. He could not let her go down for trying to help his daughter. Mel might even understand that.

"I need complete confidentiality on this, Ed."

"Sure."

"McQuaid's pissed at Jennifer because she thinks she told me the Aldrich has a cure for AIDS."

Ed tilted his head, narrowed his eyes. "What?"

Dave spoke slowly. "Liv's tested HIV positive,"

"Liv? Your daughter? How the heck did that happen?"

Squeezing his lips together, Dave shook his head. "We don't know."

"She's not that old, is she?"

"Fifteen."

Ed said nothing for a moment, his eyes boring into his top VP and likely successor. He tapped his hands on the arms of his chair.

Shifting in his chair uneasily, Dave filled the silence. "I told Claire that I'd heard the Aldrich had a cure in the oven. She denied it, but she insisted that Jennifer had told me something."

"Did she?"

"She hinted."

Ed looked at him questioningly.

"Okay, she did," Dave said. "But she was very careful. She did not say it was a certainty."

"I understand Claire's position. If one of my former employees broke a confidentiality agreement, I'd be pissed off, too. Why didn't Claire just tell me that's what this was about?"

"Maybe because that would be admitting that there is a cure in the works."

"Wouldn't that be good news for Liv?" Ed asked.

"I hope so, but I don't understand why she wouldn't tell me about it."

"C'mon, Dave. She has confidentiality issues, too. She can't tell you. I'll bet she'd probably love to help Liv."

"Why?"

"I know her. She's full of passion for her work. She lives to help people. And she thinks the world of you. But she's also a professional who knows you have to live by a set of rules to stay in position to help."

Dave sighed.

Ed continued, "Doesn't change the fact that Jennifer broke confidentiality and put Claire, and you I might add, in a very awkward spot."

Ed let this sink in while Dave pondered the mountains and considered. Jennifer thought she was helping. Plus Dave had a complete confidentiality package with the Aldrich. At worst, it was a judgment call. Firing her was inappropriate, but Ed seemed to have made up his mind, probably goaded on by comments made by Middleton. Middleton had jumped at every opportunity to get one-on-one with Ed recently, actively trying to work around Dave.

"I'm not going to fire her over this..."

Ed interrupted, "Assuming that you have the right reason for Claire's attitude."

"Right. But even without that, we're too far into this with too much at stake to cause that kind of disruption now."

"Okay, Dave. It's your call. You're important to this company. I promised you I would never micro-manage you. I'm not going to start with this issue. That's what I'll tell Claire."

Dave tapped his palms on the side of his thighs as he stood up. "Thanks, Ed. Maybe she'll tell you what's really going on."

"Maybe."

Dave started out the door.

"One other thing, Clement," Ed said. "Be a little more discreet in your meetings with this woman. No more one-on-one's in your office after most of us have gone home. And slug her next time she tries to hug you or even touch you."

The two men exchanged understanding grins.

As soon as Dave left the office, Hepp dialed Claire. He knew she would not be happy. He could barely get his fingers to hit the right buttons on the dial pad. Every moment of every day had become an effort. He did not have much time left to be effective. He and Claire agreed that Dave was still the best choice. Yet they sure as hell could not afford to let him spoil everything now.

CHAPTER 6

Cameron Pass: Aldrich High Altitude Facility
November 27, 2:40 p.m. Mountain Time

A swirling dust of snow flung a biting chill at Mike's exposed face and hands. He ducked, a forearm over his eyes for protection as he ran to the door of the chopper. In a tight brown leather coat with faux fur collar, Claire reached out to him with a gloved hand as she stepped down on to the heated helipad. The two walked quickly to the building, greeted by warm air as they entered.

"So, Farley, do you have things under control up here?"

"Yes, ma'am," Mike replied. "The boys love their work."

"No repercussions?"

"None," he said, his Irish lilt still strong after nearly a decade based in the United States.

"How are you keeping the lid on?"

"No one gets to see local papers for starters, print or online. And no one's allowed off premises. We justified that with the run-up to the late December benchmark."

Claire pulled off her gloves as she walked, her two-inch leather boot heels clicking on the concrete floor. "No whining about being here Thanksgiving?"

"Sure, but they're startin' to understand that this is a bit like a military operation. We let 'em write and talk on the phone. Keyword eavesdroppin' is workin' well."

"Did you find any infractions?"

"Minor stuff. Nothin' deliberate. Nothin' threatenin' to us. Not like Sheila."

As they entered Claire's office with its enormous window filled with silver-white mountain peaks and snow, the aroma of fresh brewed coffee filled their senses. On one wall, an enormous stone fireplace blazed orange.

"Feels like home," Claire commented. "Thank you, Mike."

They sat in two overstuffed wingbacks beside the fire. Mike poured the coffee which sat on an end table.

"I've not done a thing about Jennifer. Are ya sure that's what ya want? Nothin'?"

Claire leaned forward to put cream in her coffee. She drank it black in Boulder, but for some reason she liked it with cream up here at 10,000 feet "So far. She should never have learned about Sheila. So now she's frightened. And pissed off. She's been away from the big picture for too long. Not enough perspective."

"She thinks she could end up like Sheila if she comes back," Mike said.

"If she turns on us, she could end up like Sheila whether or not she comes back. She was completely insubordinate when I spoke with her on the phone. She could put the whole project in jeopardy."

"You're a cold one, Claire. You practically raised those two."

Claire sipped her coffee and then spoke over the rim. "I'd have myself killed if I thought I was impeding the mission. It's all about the mission."

"I'll take that as fair warning. So how do you want me to handle it?"

"She still has work to do with the Clements. Now more than ever. She's close to Dave. What if she tells him about Sheila? We need him – probably more than her - and we have to be able to control him. She has to finish tightening the circle around him. Make sure she does."

"You have my word."

"Did you crack Sheila's latest cloud upload?"

"No. It's password protected, but she didn't give Clement the password either."

"Hack it and find out what's in it."

"It's in the Amazon cloud, ma'am. It's tough to crack. Then, if we do hack it, we're inviting scrutiny from a very large corporate animal."

"What's that mean?"

"We shouldn't poke the bear. The risk associated with the potential scrutiny far outweighs the likelihood of Clement hacking her password."

Claire steepled her fingers and thought for a moment. "Okay," she said. "Do it your way. Leave it alone. For now. In any event, if Jennifer gets her job done, we'll have Dave well in hand before he figures it out."

"If he figures it out. Meanwhile, we can hope that Jennifer's a good actor and pulls off the next stage."

"Don't rely on her acting. Make her believe."

"Very interesting." Mike took a swig of his coffee. "You're tough on your protégés. I'll handle her personally."

"For the greater good," she said.

"Yes ma'am. The team will be waiting for you in the executive boardroom at 10:30. I'll go make sure things are ready."

Reaching into her small briefcase, she said, "Not yet. I have something for you."

"Oh," he said, sitting back down. "What's that?"

"There's a priest in Rome that seems a bit disenchanted with the priesthood."

"Ya found him?" Mike responded. "I'll be damned."

"That you will," Claire said without cracking a smile. She spread a handful of pictures on the coffee table. One showed Father Jim Reilly on the Pont Sant Angelo with a short, slender brunette. Another showed him pressing lire into the hand of a known member of the Red Brigade. Another placed him at a café bar chatting with the same dark-headed woman as in the first shot.

"It is him. Would ya look at that! My little brother. All dressed in his black priestly splendor."

"Pay more attention, Mike."

Mike studied the three pictures again. Things began to dawn on him. "Why is he with this woman?"

"Good question. Do you recognize the guy he's paying off?"

"No."

"Francesco Vitello. Red Brigade."

"Mother of mercy."

"Priesthood's over for him. He's trying to find you and get back to the life. The skinny girl is one of mine. She's kept us informed. He thinks he's in love with her so he tells her everything. Or at least he did. We had her break up with him to further disillusion him. She told him she could not have an affair with a priest. Said she needed something out in the open of which she could be proud. He's crestfallen. In complete denial."

"Can we get him here?"

"He paid to find out you're in the States. We'll get him that far. The rest is up to you."

"The mountain air will do him good."

Claire beamed. "You owe me, Farley," she said.

"You're a darlin', Ms. McQuaid," he said as he got up to hug her. She patted his back perfunctorily.

As Mike left the office, her eyes stared right through the back of him. When he shrugged his shoulders as though to shake her off, she knew she had him under control. She found his gratitude delightfully ironic in light of her plans for him and his brother.

From the wingback, Claire opened a small compartment and pressed three buttons in succession. The first closed and latched the door. The second caused great metal blinds to slide down over the massive windows. And the third opened a large panel in the opposite wall, disclosing a 65" HDTV plasma screen. A menu appeared on the screen. She navigated it until she found what she wanted.

A few moments later, she renewed her resolve as she watched the growing video montage of terror.

APPENDIX

ABOUT THE AUTHOR

With *Public Offerings*, Bob LiVolsi won the Writers League of Texas prestigious manuscript contest for best thriller. Bob was also a finalist in the same competition for best narrative non-fiction. He started his career as a journalist and was managing editor of the Daily Kent Stater at Kent State University. There, he won the Sears Congressional Internship for his investigative coverage of racial tension on campus.

A former high tech executive on teams that took two companies public, Bob applied his experiences in the mercenary world of high-stakes investment to Public Offerings. As a vice president with Hewlett Packard and in his roles in building new companies, he traveled the world, partnering with large corporations, governments and other international organizations. Bob has also consulted for VRI, a vaccine research start-up. His private support of missions in sub-Saharan Africa and Central America brought him closer to the day-to-day challenges presented by disease, poverty and tyranny. In the mid-1990s, he began online communication with a missionary priest in Sierra Leone where he learned about the horrors there not yet reported in the western press. The priest disappeared and was assumed killed. He became the inspiration for Fr. Jim Reilly in *Public Offerings*.

Bob LiVolsi lives in Austin, Texas, with his wife and two daughters. He is currently writing *Courtship of Innocence*, the sequel to the *Public Offerings* series.

CHARACTER SUMMARIES

Clement Family, Fort Collins, Colorado

Dave Clement

> Dave is the father of Liv Clement and husband of Mel Clement. As VP of Operations and Business Development at Prodeus, he is the main driver of partnerships to deploy the Portable DNA Analyzer (PDNA) with malaria vaccine pilot in West Africa. Dave is the likely successor to Ed Hepp as CEO of Prodeus. Claire McQuaid, Executive Director of Aldrich, relies on Dave's partnership and his relationships in the pharmaceutical industry and with international aid organizations

Liv Clement

> Fifteen year old daughter of Dave and Mel Clement. Liv is a good student and volleyball player at Ft. Collins High School where she is a sophomore. She is on anti-retrovirals to manage HIV. She insists to her parents and doctors that she has participated in no risky behaviors that would lead to HIV. She has not had a blood transfusion, another possible source of HIV. She keeps her HIV very secret; her friends, teachers, and coaches do not know she has it. She frequently writes in a diary to help her cope

Mel Clement

> Liv's mother and wife of Dave Clement. Mel works as a mortgage broker, but now seldom goes into the office, working from home to be present for Liv. Mel is frustrated with Dave for constantly prioritizing work over family and feels he is not doing enough to help find answers for Liv's HIV.

Aldrich Institute, Colorado

Claire McQuaid

Executive Director of the Boulder, Colorado-based Aldrich Institute. She has spearheaded the development of the malaria vaccine to be tested in Sierra Leone with the Lokoma tribe and others. Claire's body is disfigured from wounds incurred when she was young. She is passionate about her work and feels a duty to change the world on a grand scale. She helped put Ed Hepp and Prodeus in business where she sits on the board. She plans to have Dave Clement replace Ed as CEO when Ed's Parkinson's disease advances to the point where he cannot carry the CEO workload. Importantly, Claire relies on Dave to smooth the way for cooperation with locals in Sierra Leone and with significant allies such as Evan Conger at the World Health Organization (WHO).

Sheila Stratemeier

Lead developer for the malaria vaccine at the Aldrich Institute. Sheila works out of the Aldrich's secretive mountain lab in northern Colorado's Rawah Wilderness, high up in the mountains near the Medicine Bow Range. Sheila is troubled by the alternatives that Claire and the Aldrich are considering for deployment of the malaria vaccine; Sheila and Jennifer Winter, who works for Dave Clement at Prodeus, are close friends going back to the days when they were protégés at the Aldrich Institute fresh out of grad school.

Eldridge Perry

Director of Drug Discovery for the Aldrich Institute. Eldridge works out of the firm's mountain lab in Colorado's Rawah Wilderness. Sheila Stratemeier and Jennifer Winter both reported directly to Eldridge when they worked there together; he is still Sheila's manager today. A very secretive and mysterious man, Eldridge compartmentalizes work assignments among his researchers and developers so that no single one of them has a complete picture of the company's plans and strategy.

Lokoma Village, Sierra Leone

Fr. Jim Reilly

Irish missionary priest who serves the people of Sierra Leone. Fr. Jim feels a special fealty to Chief Hamara Karanja and the Lokoma tribe. He baptized Chief Karanja and the tribe members when they converted from a local tribal religion three years ago. He is itinerant, traveling from village to village and often saying Mass outdoors. Dave Clement and Fr. Jim have been friends since Fr. Jim gave a fundraising sermon at Dave's church in Colorado eight years ago. Since then, Dave and Mel have contributed funds and time to help the Lokoma through hard economic times during the civil war in Sierra Leone.

Hamara Karanja

Paramount chief of the Lokoma nation in the northwest mountains of Sierra Leone. Hamara considers Dave Clement a friend through Dave's efforts to bring medical missions to the Lokoma, bringing items such as eyeglasses and prescription medicines. Hamara is married to Mariama Karanja who has given birth to two daughters: Ketta and Sara. Ketta died recently at age seven from malaria. Sara is five and her family dotes on her, particularly since the loss of Ketta. Hamara's oldest child Jacob, age 10, is his son by his first wife, Ani. Hamara was married to both Ani and Mariama simultaneously, but had to choose one when he converted to Catholicism, as polygamy is outlawed by Church law. He chose Mariama. Jacob holds this against his father.

Jacob Karanja

Hamara's oldest child, Jacob was born to Hamara's estranged wife Ani. Age 10, he lives with Ani, his birth mother, in the chief's compound along with Ani's parents, Mariama and his sister Sara. Jacob aspires to be a chief like his father and seeks ways to demonstrate his manhood, but he is troubled that his father threw out his birth mother.

International Aid Organizations (NGOs)

Adrian Guerra

> The West African Country Director for the World Bank, Adrian is based in Freetown, Sierra Leone. Adrian persuades Dave Clement to place the malaria vaccine pilot in Sierra Leone, not strife-torn Nigeria. Adrian wants Chief Karanja to sell the Lokoma tribe's ancestral land to another tribe, ostensibly to get the Lokoma to more reliable medical care and safer environs in Freetown away from the criminal bands that still wander the bush, years after the official end of the civil war. Chief Karanja opposes such a move, believing he owes it to his tribe and to their ancestors to keep the Lokoma where they are. Adrian has to sign off on the World Bank funds needed to subsidize the malaria vaccine project in Sierra Leone.

Evan Conger

> Director of sub-Saharan tropical diseases for the World Health Organization (WHO), Evan is a reliable and experienced hand in health care administration and drug discovery. He served as Executive Director of the Aldrich Institute until the President of the United States tapped him to be Surgeon General. After serving in the administration, he could not go back to the Aldrich where Claire McQuaid was doing an effective job as his replacement. Instead, he took the job at WHO, hoping to make a difference there, particularly with regard to malaria. He started the malaria vaccine research at the Aldrich and is working with Dave Clement to bring the pilot project for the vaccine to Sierra Leone. WHO's endorsement of the effort will be critical to its deployment and its financial success. Evan and Dave have known each other for years and have a close, trusting relationship. Evan is the kind of man everyone looks up to as a mentor.

Author's Note

On the next page is a short bibliography where more information can be found about what the situation on the ground is really like in West Africa. Much of the developing world remains in turmoil, facing daily trials that those in the developed countries may rarely, if ever, encounter. Thanks to the Gates Foundation, The World Health Organization, Doctors Without Borders, pharmaceutical firms (big and small) and others, including many small faith-based NGOs, help is reaching many of the people. But not nearly enough. And stability is extremely difficult to maintain.

Some true-to-life facts mentioned in the Public Offerings series:

- Many in the region really believe that vaccines are a western plot delivering HIV and infertility.
- One in five children in Sierra Leone dies before age five.
- So-called rebel bands still roam the bush even where civil war has ended, and civil wars are still ongoing or brewing. Maiming, murder and rape are common in these situations.
- The Boko Haram in Nigeria and extreme elements of both Christian and Islamic groups in the Central African Republic keep life dangerous and short in their respective countries.
- A form of AIDS that kills at an accelerated rate has been discovered in West Africa.
- There is, in fact, evidence that a malaria vaccine may cause more virulent strains of malaria: Mackinnon MJ, Read AF (2004) Immunity Promotes Virulence Evolution in a Malaria Model. PLoS Biol 2(9): e230. doi:10.1371/journal.pbio.0020230; http://www.plosbiology.org/article/info%3Adoi%2F10.1371%2Fj ournal.pbio.0020230
- Sierra Leone, according to many studies, remains the poorest nation on the planet.

Some Selected Readings:

Nigeria Polio Vaccine Workers Killed, Boko Haram Suspected
http://www.huffingtonpost.com/2013/02/08/nigeria-polio-vaccine-
workers-killed_n_2647539.html

MalariaVaccine.Org: The website for the Path Malaria Vaccine Initiative

Newly Discovered HIV Strain, A3/02, Linked With Faster Development of
AIDS
http://www.huffingtonpost.com/2013/12/02/new-hiv-strain-a3-02-
development-aids_n_4372428.html

A Long Way Gone: Memoirs of a Boy Soldier by Ishmael Beah –
Autobiography of a former child soldier in Sierra Leone, Farrar Strauss &
Giroux 2008; also Ishmael's website:
http://www.alongwaygone.com/index.html

Sierra Leone: Treating Malaria in Children
http://www.doctorswithoutborders.org/article/sierra-leone-treating-
malaria-children

World Health Organization Website on Sierra Leone:
http://www.who.int/countries/sle/en/

Rigzone for news about Oil in West Africa:
http://www.rigzone.com/news/oil_gas/r/3/West_Africa

IRIN Humanitarian News and Analysis Sierra Leone:
http://www.irinnews.org/country/sl/sierra-leone

International AIDS Vaccine initiative:
http://www.iavi.org/Pages/default.aspx

The River: A Journey to the Source of HIV and AIDS by Edward Cooper,
Little, Brown & Co 1999

Polio Eradication Initiative: Challenges in polio and politics of Nigeria:
http://www.polioeradication.org/Infectedcountries/Nigeria.aspx

Sierra Leone Demographic and Health Survey Key Findings 2008:
http://www.measuredhs.com/pubs/pdf/sr171/sr171.pdf

Sierra Leone Still Suffers Legacy of Child Soldiers:
http://www.ipsnews.net/2012/04/sierra-leone-still-suffers-legacy-of-child-soldiers/

Oil Pirates and the Mystery Ship:
http://www.foreignpolicy.com/articles/2014/01/28/oil_pirates_and_the_mystery_ship

The West African Oil and Gas Market 2013-2023:
http://www.marketwatch.com/story/the-west-african-oil-gas-market-2013-2023-2013-09-18

Public Offerings continues in

Public Offerings Book Three:

Killer Priest

You can buy each of the four books in the Public Offerings series at your favorite book store in either eBook or print format.

Or you can purchase all four books and get the complete Public Offerings series in a single volume at your favorite bookstore, including the Amazon Kindle bookstore at http://goo.gl/MdkLFY

Public Offerings Book 1:   Birthright

Public Offerings Book 2: The Price of a Life

Public Offerings Book 3:   Killer Priest

Public Offerings Book 4:   Children on the Altar

Public Offerings Complete: All Four Books in One Volume

Learn more: www.PublicOfferings.net

Follow: www.Facebook.com/PublicOfferings